Trans Imagination

C. M. Jacqline

ISBN: 978-1-955348-02-7

Trans Imagination

C. M. Jacqline

In Loving Memory

In loving memory of my mom and dad, Eleanor and Jonathan, who always supported and encouraged my siblings and me to develop our abilities, to explore our talents and to pursue our dreams.

Dedication

I dedicate this book to the first person with whom I shared that I am transgender.

My brother, John, better known to family and friends as Butch, who was not only my brother, he was also my best friend. Butch passed away in 2004. His love and support for me never wavered. It remained strong when I told him I was transgender. Butch was steadfast in his feelings until the day he died. I miss him dearly.

Acknowledgement

I thank my friend, Linda Hill, for her devotion and editing skills in helping me to complete this book and, equally important, for helping me to fulfill my dream.

Imaginings

Cassie

Summer was over and Cassie was finally able to spend her first day at the beach by herself. She was thrilled at the excitement of having healed from a very successful gender affirmation surgery. Cassie had been born a boy but always identified being a girl and thanks to the love and support of her mother was able to transition.

That is not to say that her life growing up was a bed of roses because it was anything but easy. Even in places, like the school she attended, she was ridiculed and treated like a non-person. As a result, the verbal abuse she had endured from other students caused her much mental anguish. Cassie's physical problems had plagued her for all of her life and yet, in spite of it all, she grew up to be a fine young lady.

Now that her surgery was complete, she knew the world she lived in would be different. It was like having both of her deepest wishes come true. One, of course, was her surgery and the second was being able to enjoy the beach once again.

The thought of being alone, soaking in the intoxicating atmosphere without interruption, was a fairy tale come true. Before leaving the narrow path, she paused and breathed in deeply, letting the clean salt air and the distinct smells of marsh grass and seaweed fill her lungs. With sandals in hand, she stepped into the soft, dry sand and giggled as it squished up between her toes and surrounded them.

After frolicking for some time, Cassie strolled toward the water's edge and marveled at the change in the texture of the sand. Unlike the warm dry area, the wet sand was cool, compact and firm against her feet. Again, she momentarily paused, this time relishing the sound of the waves gently lapping the shore in an alluring, tranquil rhythm. She took a couple steps until the water was above her ankles and lifted her arms up to the sky while tilting her face toward the sun. As Cassie stood there, she delighted at the fantasy of miraculously becoming one with the ocean.

A woman's sudden, desperate cry for help yanked Cassie out of her daydream. Without a moment's hesitation, she scurried in the direction of the woman's screams.

"Help me, please!" the woman screamed louder when she spotted Cassie. "My husband choked on a piece of meat and passed out. I don't know what to do."

Cassie jammed her hand in her beach bag and pulled out her cell phone. "Here, call 911," she commanded, then dropped to her knees and turned the man onto his side. When she got his mouth open, she gave a few sharp whacks in between the man's shoulder blades. Nothing happened.

She stuck her small hand in as far as possible. Luckily, her fingers reached the edge of the meat and she was able to hook it with her fingernails. She gently pulled and was able to dislodge the chunk from his throat. Wasting no time, she rolled the man onto his back and immediately felt for the carotid artery in his neck while at the same time listened for breathing. Finding neither, she hurriedly began performing CPR.

After some very tense minutes, the man responded. Then, as if having been behind the small sand dune, the EMTs appeared almost instantaneously. They wasted no time taking the man's vital signs. They assured the woman that they believed her husband would be okay but needed to transport him to the hospital just to be certain.

Knowing the couple was in good hands, Cassie slipped away and decided she had had enough excitement for one day and headed home. Not long after, there was a knock on the door, and when Cassie's mother answered it, she was taken aback upon seeing two EMTs standing there. Puzzled, she asked, "Can I help you?"

One of the men stepped forward. "I'm sorry to bother you, maam, but does a young girl Cassie live here?"

Cassie's mother glanced over her shoulder at her daughter then turned back to him. Holding her hands against her chest in fear that something was wrong with Cassie she said, "Yes, that's my daughter. I'm Mrs. Adderson. Is something wrong with her?"

"No. No there's nothing wrong with Cassie. Forgive me. My name is Dan and this is my partner Jim. May we come in so we can explain?"

Not knowing what to think, Mrs. Adderson stepped aside and invited them in. "What's this all about? Did something go wrong with Cassie's surgery? She's transgender and just went through gender affirmation surgery."

Dan put up his hand. "It's nothing like that at all." Once inside, Dan held up Cassie's bag. "Your daughter left this on the beach. We found her wallet inside with this address."

Confused, she said, "So EMTs patrol the beach now and they had to send the two of you to return a beach bag?"

Dan shook his head and smiled. "No. We were called to the scene on the beach about a man who had choked on a piece of meat."

Somewhat at a loss, Mrs. Adderson said, "So what does this have to do with Cassie?"

Jim stepped forward. "Mrs. Adderson, your daughter saved that man's life."

"What?" blurted Mrs. Adderson incredulously. "My Cassie? You're telling me my Cassie saved someone's life?"

Both Dan and Jim nodded.

Mrs. Adderson shook her head as though trying to shake all the chaotic thoughts into a coherent message. "But how? I don't understand how that could be."

"You should be very proud of her," Dan said pointing to Cassie.

"I am proud of her," Mrs. Adderson replied. "But you say she saved a man's life?"

"She did," replied Dan. "In fact, if she hadn't responded as quickly as she had he more than likely would have died before we got there. Or, at best he'd be in a vegetative state from brain damage. Your daughter is a hero."

Still in a stupor like state, Mrs. Adderson shook her head again. "You don't know the half of it."

She turned toward Cassie, and when she did, the contents of Cassie's bag accidentally spilled out onto the floor. It was then that Dan and Jim spotted the folding white cane and discovered Cassie was blind.

Crystal Clear

Kelly's eyes darted to the clock above the desk when she heard the key sliding into the lock, and cursed for having lost track of time. She scrambled to get all her notes jammed into her folder before Todd, her fiancé, walked into the room. She was just putting the last scrap of paper into the folder when Todd entered.

"What's that?" Todd asked seeing Kelly's expression and the way she was clutching the folder to her chest.

"Nothing really," she said rather nonchalantly, hoping her casual manner would dismiss the subject then and there.

"It's more than that. You're working on another story aren't you?" he said, his eyes shifting to the folder.

Kelly's fingers tightened on the folder as if she were protecting the contents. She wished she had better control of her emotions. With a slight smile, she said, "Not really a story, just an idea for a story if I can sort it all out."

"What's it about?"

"I'm not really sure. Like I said it's just an idea."

"Have you written any of it yet?" he asked, his eyes still lingering on the folder.

She knew if she said no he wouldn't believe her because of the way she gripped the folder so tightly, a sure sign it was a work in progress. At the same time, however, she didn't dare tell him it was near completion; not because she was ashamed of it, but because he would hound her to read it and that was the one thing she couldn't allow......ever.

"Yes, I've written a few pages, but, like I said, it's just rough ideas and nothing really coherent to base a story on yet."

"Oh, okay," he said and turned to walk into the kitchen.

Kelly breathed a sigh of relief.

Todd turned to her. "After I get myself a sandwich, I'll come back and read what you've written and tell you what I think."

"No!" she snapped too harshly before she could stop herself. Deep inside she

4

knew that that was the biggest mistake she could have ever made.

Todd faced her and tilted his head to the side. "What's going on, Kelly? You've never stopped me from reading your material before. What are you hiding?"

"I'm not hiding anything," she lied. "It's just that…..well it's just that I don't want to jinx the story if, and I stress, 'if', there is a story there. Nor do I want any of my ideas influenced by something you might say."

"It's never bothered you before. In fact, some of the things I've suggested in the past opened up more ideas and made your stories a little better. You said so yourself."

"Not this one," she replied and got up from the desk.

Todd shook his head in disbelief from what he was hearing. "Are you having an affair and writing a journal or a story based upon your exploits? Is that why you don't want me to see it?"

Kelly spun on her heels. "Oh don't be so damn ridiculous. No, I am not having an affair and this is not anything like that. Why do people always jump to conclusions of cheating and secret rendezvous? It's just a story about…"

"A story about what?" he asked, walking towards her.

"It's just an idea. I told you that."

"You admitted it was a story a minute ago."

"It….it slipped out that way. I'm so used to saying story I wasn't even aware I had said it."

Todd studied her for a long moment. "All right, Kelly, have it your way, but I want you to know I'm aware that you're lying to me. For whatever reason, I haven't a clue, but I know you are not being truthful with me." He turned and stormed out of the room.

Kelly's eyes brimmed with tears knowing that what she had just done would surely put the trust in their relationship in jeopardy. She had always been honest with him. Right from the beginning, when they first met, she told him she's a pre-op transgender male-to-female person striving to fulfill her life through gender affirming surgery. To his credit, Todd looked beyond her physical anatomy and accepted her for her. He always assured Kelly that he fell in love with her for her personality and tender and compassionate heart. The only thing she could hope for was that in time the wound caused by the mistrust she had just created would heal and they would be happy again. Like most transgender people, Kelly knew only too well the difficulties a transgender person faces when trying to find someone who will accept and love them. She glanced down at the folder still clutched in her hands and let the tears flow.

It felt like her heart was being ripped apart. On the one hand, if she didn't let Todd read what she had written, he would be deeply hurt and possibly never forgive her or trust her again. It was equally possible their relationship would be destroyed. On the other hand, if she did let him read it, their relationship would definitely be destroyed forever. What to do?

She plopped down into the swivel rocker near the window and glanced out at the dreary overcast sky; a perfect reflection of how she felt. There was no sense reprimanding herself for having been so careless. It wouldn't serve any purpose to do so since the damage was already done.

Her eyes drifted to the folder. The same question that had come into her mind over and over and over again since sitting down to write the story two weeks earlier reared its head once again. "Why am I so compelled to write such a story, and so driven to finish it so quickly?" she asked herself. As with all the other times, she had no answer other than the speculation that she had somehow become possessed, which was something she didn't subscribe to at all. Yet somehow, that's exactly what she seemed to be feeling since the story's inception. Whatever the reason for her compulsion to write the story, it was imperative she completely destroy it when it was finished. Under no circumstances could she allow anyone to read it, especially Todd.

Kelly closed her eyes and thought of Todd. A steady stream of tears coursed down her cheeks. She lay back and wished with all her heart that she could go back in time to before the compulsion to write the story began. Pulling herself from the chair, she made her way to the bed and crawled into the center of it. She turned on her side, crushed the folder against her chest, and curled up into a fetal position.

The sound of the door opening and closing and the lock being turned caught her attention and she knew Todd wouldn't be back that night. She cried long hard tears. As darkness crept into the room, her tears ceased and she took deep slow breaths to relax.

It wasn't long before another set of questions invaded her thoughts. "Why didn't I throw the story away once I realized the consequences? Why don't I destroy it knowing what would befall the reader? Why am I so insanely driven to finish it even now? Why am I not strong enough to resist it?" Of course, there were no answers, or at least none that satisfied her.

Mulling it over in her mind, Kelly tried desperately to think of a solution to her dilemma. She bolted upright, the folder flying from her hands, scattering pages and notes across the floor. Panic gripped her tightly until she felt as though she couldn't breathe. Without a second glance at the papers strewn about the floor, Kelly jumped up from the bed and started pacing back and forth.

"Oh my God," she cried out to the darkness. "What if it can't be destroyed?"

The thought was so crippling it buckled her knees and she fell to the floor. She pulled herself to the bed and slowly stood up. Frightened as she had never been before, Kelly moved to the wall and flipped the switch, thankful for the light that instantly flooded the room. She went into the other rooms and turned on all the lights. That done, she went to the kitchen cupboards to look for the small jar of coffee she kept there for times like this.

Behind a large mixing bowl, Kelly discovered an unopened bottle of Hennessy. She didn't normally drink alcohol, but thought it just might calm her nerves. She grabbed the bottle, snatched up a cup, sat at the table and poured a healthy portion of liquor into the cup.

Less than a quarter of the way through the bottle, Kelly noticed her reflection in

the hallway mirror and laughed loudly. Continuing to look at her image, she said, "Are you happy now I've gone insane?" She laughed again and took another mouthful of cognac.

"This is stupid. It's a story, Kelly," she scolded herself. "It's a damn story! It's nothing but words on paper. There's nothing to be afraid of."

She stood up and unsteadily walked toward the mirror. Pointing her finger at her likeness, Kelly said, "You scared the wits out of me; you know that? You wrote the story and you would never hurt anyone, so there can't be anything wrong with it. Are you paying attention to me? You better, because if you don't you're going to lose Todd forever and I'll never forgive you. You hear me, Kelly? I said I'll never forgive you if you cause me to lose Todd."

Kelly emptied the glass. Feeling wobbly, she leaned against the opposite wall and smiled. "Don't look so smug. I'm the one who figured it out, not you. And for your information, it doesn't matter why I felt obsessed to finish it because that just shows I have a deep passion when I have a good story to write."

Having soothed her conscience, Kelly pushed herself from the wall and took a step toward the table. She half-turned to look into the mirror again. "Oh yeah, I almost forgot. I'm letting Todd read the story as soon as I finish it. How do you like those apples? I know I'm drunk but I'm still letting him read it."

Making her way into the bedroom, Kelly flopped down on the bed. Moments later, she passed out and didn't wake up until late the next morning.

When she woke up, Kelly moaned and slowly opened her eyes. She quickly squeezed them shut again to block out the bright morning sun beaming through the large window. Her mouth was as dry as cotton. She forced herself to get up and shuffled into the bathroom, thankful she didn't have a hangover. Once refreshed and dressed, Kelly walked into the kitchen and spotted the half-empty bottle on the table.

"Thanks for your help, Pal," she smirked, recalling her one-sided conversation with her reflection. Glancing at the mirror, Kelly almost expected to see her image still posed with a smug look on her face. She moved closer to the mirror and smiled. "I remember everything from last night, and I meant what I said about letting Todd read it when it's finished."

Although she didn't have a hangover, Kelly didn't press her luck by eating a big breakfast. Instead, she settled for a small bowl of cereal. Thoughts of her actions and feelings over the past weeks infiltrated her mind and she shook her head, thinking how foolish she had been. Instead of hurrying to wash the dishes as soon a she finished the cereal, Kelly lingered at the table a while longer, hoping some light would be shed on why she had acted the way she did. The only thing that came to mind was that she had simply gotten overzealous with the story and somehow allowed it to take over her life.

With coffee mug in hand, she went into the bedroom, picked up all her notes and pages, and then started sorting them out on the bed. Once she was organized, Kelly sat at her desk and read the last pages she had written. Nothing new came to

mind, so she closed her eyes and concentrated on clearing away all thoughts to allow her creative juices to flow. It didn't take long for her imagination to kick in and, before long, she had five pages completed and only had to write the ending.

Writing the ending, however, proved to be more difficult to write than she had first thought. No matter how hard she tried, she just couldn't get the words to flow. After several failed attempts and completely frustrated, Kelly put the pen down and stared at the blank sheet of paper. Ten minutes later, she stood up, grabbed the mug and stepped into the kitchen to get more coffee.

Looking over her shoulder at the papers on the desk she said, "How could you do this to me? How could you let me get all the way to the end and then give me a brain fart? Aaaaagh! It's not fair."

Two painstaking hours passed with no satisfactory results. Each time she thought it was finished, Kelly would read it over and decide it wasn't quite right. The story demanded a strong ending. Somehow, she had lost the feeling for the story and decided to take a break and run some errands.

She stopped at a gas station and filled the tank. Just as she was leaving, her phone rang. She quickly glanced at the screen and saw that it was from her friend Paula.

"Hi, Paula!" she greeted cheerily.

"Hey, kiddo, what are you up to? Haven't heard from you in some time now?"

"I'm sorry, Paula. I got so wrapped up in my writing I just lost track of time."

"Another story......that's fantastic! What's it about?"

"Are you free for lunch?" Kelly asked, avoiding Paula's question.

"Yeah, you want to come here or meet some place?"

"How about we meet at Shirley's Diner?" Kelly suggested.

"Sounds great," Paula replied happily. "Meet you there in fifteen."

"Great," Kelly said and ended the call.

Twenty minutes later, Kelly entered the diner and spotted Paula in a booth toward the back of the restaurant.

"I ordered you a coffee," Paula said as soon as Kelly slid into the booth. "So, tell me what the story's about."

"Hello to you, too," Kelly said as she raised her cup to her lips.

Paula laughed. "We said hello half an hour ago on the phone. Tell me about the story."

Kelly set the cup down and looked into Paula's eyes. "Okay. Before I do, let me tell you how the idea for the story came about and what's happened since then. You're probably not going to believe it when I tell you. Hell, I don't believe it myself, but it happened."

Kelly proceeded to tell Paula the events that led up to the idea for the story. She explained as best she could about strange happenings afterwards. She emphasized how she was so obsessed with the story that she couldn't really eat or sleep restfully.

Not knowing Kelly was having lunch with Paula, Todd decided to take half a day off from work so he could go back to the apartment and straighten things out with her. The main thing he wanted to do was to apologize for having insinuated that she would stoop so low as to cheat on him. In his heart, he knew full well that was something Kelly would never do. He was angry with himself for having let his temper get the best of him. He loved her completely. She was the most beautiful person he had ever met, and he was looking forward to one day marrying her.

He couldn't even say with any conviction that he felt hurt that she didn't want him to read the story. It wasn't so life-changing or threatening that it should have bothered him the way it had. Try as he might, he couldn't figure out why he had had such an outburst. Whatever the reason, he wanted to apologize and make things right with her.

"Kelly," Todd called out as soon as he entered the apartment. "Listen, I want to apologize for my remarks last night. They were way out of line and I never should've said what I did."

He went into the bedroom and, not seeing her there, checked all the other rooms, calling her name as he went. It wasn't unusual for her to be out in the afternoon, but after the past two weeks of hardly leaving her desk, it seemed strange to not see her there writing.

Without further thought, Todd made a coffee and stood by the kitchen counter drinking it. He carried the cup into the bedroom and looked out the window at the parking lot to see if Kelly had returned. He waited a few minutes, and then turned to walk back to the kitchen.

On his way out of the room, Todd glanced at Kelly's desk and saw the open folder with all the pages in it. At first, he took a few steps, but then stopped. Looking over his shoulder at the open folder, he spun on his heels and went over to the desk. He fingered the pages and read a few lines on each page.

Before he knew it, Todd was sitting down engrossed in the story. He wasn't an editor or an expert in the writing field, but he knew good writing when he read it. He also believed it was the best story Kelly had ever written, and almost felt guilty for reading it without her permission. At the same time, now that he was gripped by the story, he couldn't put it down. He flipped to the back page, looked at the page number then glanced at his watch. Todd figured he could finish it in a relatively short period of time.

Before he started back in on the story, thoughts of how Kelly had gotten upset with his wanting to read it before it was finished sprung into his mind. Now he understood why. It was a compelling story. He recalled her words that she was afraid he would jinx it and somehow it seemed right. She must have sensed that it was her best story and didn't want anything or anyone to interfere with her creation.

Midway through the story, Todd felt a strange sensation wash over him and sat back in the chair. Almost as fast as the feeling came, it passed. He continued reading. He had read many stories before but none as compelling and interesting as the one he held in his hands. Not because it was written by Kelly, but because it was a genuinely fantastic story in its own right.

A few pages later, he felt strange again, and leaned back in the chair. He didn't feel sick, just weird. He wasn't dizzy, queasy or even lightheaded. He picked up his coffee and stared at it wondering if there was something wrong with it. Lifting the cup, he took a small taste and didn't detect anything out of the ordinary. In fact, it tasted real good.

Once again, the feeling passed and Todd began reading again. He was amazed and impressed with Kelly's ability to write. He couldn't help pause every now and then to think about her creative genius, and wondered why he had never realized it before. One thing was certain, he would do everything in his power to help her get the story published.

Todd flipped to the next page and knew he was nearly finished. He glanced at the words and wondered how the story would end. He devoured and absorbed every word, letting each one work its way into his mind. They created a picture so vivid and feelings so real, he couldn't believe it was just a story.

He tried to turn the next page and realized he couldn't feel the paper and thought his hand had fallen asleep. Lifting his arm, he shook it to wake it up. But instead of getting the pins and needles sensation, nothing happened. Todd looked at his hand as though he was staring at an alien being's hand. He tried willing it into action to no avail. It was then that the fear reared its head. He jammed his working hand into his pocket for his phone to call Kelly, thought better of it, and pulled his hand back out. He couldn't call her. What would she say? What would he say? He'd sound like a lunatic. Besides, it couldn't be real. He glanced at the clock and knew she'd probably be home soon.

For the first time in days, Kelly was filled with excitement. It felt fantastic to finally be able to tell someone about the story. She looked at Paula and smiled. "You can't imagine how good I feel right now. It's like a ton of bricks has been lifted from my shoulders."

Paula returned the smile, happy to be a part of Kelly's liberation. "So it really gripped you that much?" she asked, trying to understand what Kelly had told her.

"Gripped me is putting it mildly. At times, you would have thought I was chained to the desk and forced to write against my will. Yet, there was something so powerful and so fulfilling about writing it. I loved it. Can you understand that?"

Paula stared at her friend and shook her head. "No I can't understand it. If you really want to know what I think, I think you've pushed yourself too far. It's either that or you've lost some of your marbles."

Kelly laughed. "I think for those few weeks, I had, but I'm over it now." She raised her coffee cup, "To the final chapter."

Paula touched her cup to Kelly's, "To the final chapter and sanity." She set the cup down and rubbed her finger around the top edge. "And this whole idea came to you after visiting that South American exhibit?"

"Yeah, can you believe it?" Kelly smiled.

Tilting her head, Paula said, "No, I can't believe it. What about the so-called curse

or whatever it was? I mean, how did you come across it and interpret it?"

"I didn't."

"What do you mean you didn't?"

"I made it all up. It's not even a real language."

"Let me get this straight. You made up a language; said it was a curse or whatever; then scared yourself into thinking it was going to happen?"

Kelly nodded and laughed. "That's it."

"Whatever possessed you to write such a story?"

"I don't know," Kelly said. She shrugged her shoulders. "It's weird because I was at the museum checking out the South American exhibit, and when I got home, I had an insatiable urge to write a story. Before I could even give it some thought, I started writing it. It was almost as if I couldn't stop myself from doing it. I can't explain it any better than that. It's crazy, huh?"

"Yeah it is," Paula agreed, then looking at her watch she said, "I gotta get going? Are you gonna be okay?"

Kelly smiled. "I'll be fine." She noticed Paula studying her, so she added, "I'll be fine. I promise."

They got up, hugged and gave each other a kiss on the cheek. "Call me," Paula said as she turned to leave. "And finish the story. I want to read it."

"I will," Kelly said to Paula's back as she left the restaurant. In the car, Kelly believed she would be okay because the compulsive feeling to spend her every waking minute writing the story was gone. The thought of finishing the story and making amends with Todd brought a smile to her lips and warmed her heart.

Pulling into the parking lot, Kelly was thrilled to see Todd's car in his parking slot. She checked herself in the mirror and said, "Okay, how do I handle this? I know, I'll let him say what he has to say and take it from there. That's it."

She opened the door, slid one leg out and pulled it back in. "No, that's not it. I should apologize first to show I think he's more important." She nodded her head and looked straight into the mirror. "He is important, and it's the right thing to do. There, it's settled."

She got out of the car and hurried to the building and was happy to see one of the elevators was already on the bottom floor. Kelly pushed number 8 and willed the door to close immediately. It had a mind of its own and took its sweet time closing even though she kept stabbing the "close door" button.

As soon as the doors opened on the eighth floor, Kelly hurried out of the elevator, turned right and quickly walked to the end of the hall. She paused in front of her door and took a few deep breaths before turning the key in the lock. She opened the door and stepped inside. She set her pocketbook on the kitchen table, looked at her appearance in the mirror, fixed her hair then walked into the bedroom.

At first, Kelly's mind didn't comprehend what she was seeing, but once it cleared and she knew what she was looking at, she froze. She couldn't believe her eyes. Somehow, her mind cleared away the fog and she half-screamed, then fainted.

She was unconscious for only a couple of minutes before hearing the sound of a distant voice calling her, willing her forward. As she came closer to awakening, Kelly recognized Todd's voice and was relieved that he had come to her rescue.

Kelly's eyelids fluttered then opened. She groggily panned the room searching for Todd.

"That's it," Todd encouraged her. "Are you okay?"

Kelly concentrated on focusing her eyes and shifted them to the sound. She opened her mouth to scream but Todd's hand covered it.

"It's me. Please don't scream Kelly. I need your help. Please, try to stay calm."

She grabbed at his hand.

"Kelly, listen to me. I don't want to die. Help me!"

The word "die" penetrated her mind and caused her to squeeze his hand. Instead of squeezing hers, Todd's hand loosened, and then released hers.

"What happened?" she managed to whisper.

"I came home early to apologize and spotted your story on the desk and started reading it and then…..and then…." Todd cleared his throat. "And then this happened. What's going on Kelly? Please help me and tell me what's happening to me?"

Kelly sat up just as Todd's strong hands lifted her to her feet. "Oh my God Todd, what have I done?"

Todd gripped her by the shoulders. "Kelly I need you to concentrate. Things are happening to me and I don't think I have much longer to live."

Kelly's eyes filled with tears. "You weren't supposed to read it. Then the more I thought about it, the more I believed it would be okay. I figured it's only a story, but it's not just a story, and now I'm afraid I'm going to lose you."

"What are you talking about?" Todd demanded. "You know what's happening to me? You knew this would happen?"

Kelly nodded then shook her head. "Yes, and….and no. I don't know."

Todd led her to a chair. He knelt down in front of her. "Kelly, look at me. Tell me what you know. It's important you tell me everything and please hurry."

Kelly told him everything she had told Paula about the story and about her fears of letting anyone read the story, especially him, but how she decided it would be okay and now her worst fears had come to life.

Todd listened attentively, and then said, "That's all of it?"

Kelly nodded.

Todd moved to the other kitchen chair and sat down. He put his head in his hands and sifted through Kelly's words, hoping to find the answer that would keep him from dying.

Kelly forced herself to focus on the situation at hand and desperately tried to think of any details she might have forgotten to mention to Paula or Todd. She wiped the tears trickling down her cheeks. Looking at Todd made her want to cry all the more, but she knew if she were to keep him alive she would have to come up with a solution.

She cleared her throat and very softly said, "Do you think if I were to go back to the museum I could get an answer?"

"We have to try," was all Todd said in an equally soft voice.

Without saying another word, Kelly rose from the chair, grabbed her keys and pocketbook and headed out the apartment. She moved along the hallway in a dazed-like state oblivious to the other people in the hallway and elevator.

Outside, the fresh air snapped her back to the moment and she rushed to her car, knowing that time was of the essence. Kelly had no idea what she was going to do once she got to the museum other than to try to repeat what she had done the first time. Unlike when she first started to write the story, she now felt compelled to help Todd in the only way she believed would help. She was certain the answer would be there waiting for her.

Thankful for the light traffic, Kelly drove with reckless abandon to the museum. Her heart pounded in her chest as she practically ran through the corridor to the room with the exhibit. She scanned the room hoping to see the statue where she had sat the day she got the idea for the story. Two people were seated on the small bench, so Kelly stood directly in front of the statue wishing she would get a feeling or idea of what to do.

She checked her watch. Ten minutes had passed and nothing had happened. Believing it was due to being too stressed out, she closed her eyes and concentrated on the meditation exercises she had taken earlier in the year. Moments later, her body relaxed and she breathed in slowly. When nothing special overcame her, Kelly silently cried, "What have I done?"

She waited an additional ten minutes. Feeling nothing like she had that first day, Kelly left the museum. Tear-filled eyes, forced her to drive much slower going home. Thoughts of Todd dying invaded every nook and cranny of her mind. She had all she could do to keep the tears at bay.

Having no idea what she would find when she entered the apartment, Kelly took a deep breath and tried to brace herself for the worst. Todd was lying on the bed. She bit her lip and walked to his side. "Honey?" she said, her words barely audible. "Can you hear me?"

Todd opened his eyes. The look on Kelly's face and her tear stained cheeks told the whole story. "It's okay," he said moving his hand to touch hers.

Kelly choked back the heavy tears fighting to break free. "I'm so sorry, Todd. I tried and tried. I failed. Oh God, how I tried." The dam burst. Kelly slumped to her knees crying. "I ….I…….I don't know…..what….to do. Todd, I don't know what to do."

Todd managed to reach and stroke her hair. "It's not your fault, Hon. Not your fault."

Kelly clutched his hand in hers and kissed it. "It is my fault. I wrote the story. It's my fault." She got to her feet and ran from the room.

How could she ever forgive herself? Why had this happened to Todd? How could a fictional story become real and destroy her whole life? They were questions that held no answers. Feeling drained and lightheaded, she staggered to the kitchen chair, sat down and buried her head in her arms.

Forty-three minutes had passed when Kelly awoke with a start. She rushed to the bedroom. Todd was sleeping. She shivered at the sight. His body was crystallizing and it was now up to his chest. She could see the organs in his body still functioning. Inasmuch as she was glad they hadn't been affected, she couldn't help but wonder why. Unable to look at him in that condition for too long, she averted her eyes. The other consolation she had was knowing that because Todd's organs were still working, she would have more time to try to find a solution.

She turned and spotted the open folder on her desk, the pages of the story were where Todd had left off reading them. Kelly moved to the desk and picked up the pages thinking that if she destroyed them Todd would return to normal. She began tearing them apart then stopped.

Something inside her told her not to do it. For a few minutes, Kelly battled with herself. On the one hand, she hated the story because of what it had done. She wanted to be rid of it once and for all. On the other hand, she feared that if she destroyed it, it would obliterate her chances to save Todd. She dropped the folder on the desk and started pacing back and forth. "What to do? What to do?" she agonized.

Kelly remembered the bottle of Hennessey and went into the kitchen. She had never truly needed a drink in her life before, but this was the exception. She needed something to take the edge off the mounting tension. She snagged the bottle from the cupboard, and without wasting time to get a glass, took a long pull. She took another swallow and placed the bottle on the counter.

It didn't take long for the Hennessey to work its magic. Kelly moved to her desk and began writing. She believed she could change the outcome by writing an entirely different ending. As with so many other things involving the story, she knew she couldn't revise what had already been written. How she knew that to be true, she had no idea. Kelly had no other choice but to write something new.

Once totally focused, Kelly immersed herself in the story and wrote page after page. The biggest challenge was creating a reverse curse using the same made-up language she had used to create the original curse. When she finished, Kelly sat back and read what she had written, wondering if the words she had penned would do the trick. It would have to do because there were no more ideas left for her to write. If the miracle was to happen, it would have to be with what she had just completed.

Hoping Todd was still alive, she picked the papers up and brought them to the bed. She forced herself to look at his chest. She could see his heart still beating and breathed a sigh of relief. "Todd, can you hear me?"

Getting no response, she touched his shoulder. "Todd, I wrote a new ending to the story. You have to read it so the spell can be reversed. Please, Todd. Please open your eyes."

Todd didn't respond and Kelly had all she could do to keep from panicking.

Instead, she climbed into bed next to him so that her mouth was close to his ear and began reading the story. She had no way of knowing if this would work, and worried what she would do if he were to die.

When Kelly finished reading, she waited and anxiously watched to see if any changes were taking place. Every second that went by seemed like an hour. She prayed with all her heart that whatever spirit or force that had made the curse come true, would now have mercy and reverse it.

With each tick of the clock, and no visible signs of improvement, Kelly's strength and hope waned. She was drained and losing her own will to live. Without Todd, her life would be meaningless. She wished beyond all hope for the curse to be removed from Todd. It had to be successful, otherwise, she would never be able to forgive herself, and that would be her demise.

Completely exhausted and her emotions sapped, Kelly closed her eyes and drifted into a deep sleep.

Somewhere in the distance, Kelly could hear voices and slowly opened her eyes. At first, she couldn't see anything. She closed and opened them again and realized Todd was not next to her. She turned her head and spotted him sitting in a chair.

"Todd," she said but no sound came out. Her mouth was dry so she worked her tongue to create some saliva. In a whispery voice she called out to him again. "Todd! Todd!"

Hearing a faint sound, Todd looked toward the bed and noticed Kelly's eyes were open. He rushed to her side. "Kelly, can you hear me?"

"You're not dead? You're alive," she said, attempting to reach out to him.

"Yes, yes," Todd said, tears of joy streaming down his cheeks.

"The curse was reversed?" Kelly asked.

Todd looked at her strangely. "I don't know anything about a curse except the one that's had you in a coma for the last six months. So yes, it has been reversed."

It was Kelly's turn to be confused. "Coma? What coma? What are you talking about? You were cursed and crystallizing… and transforming into a crystal statue… and it was my fault."

Again, Todd didn't understand what she was referring to and squeezed her hand. "As you can see, I'm not crystallizing. You had your gender affirming surgery six months ago and it was a complete success. But then you caught some kind of virus that was going around, and the only way the doctors could save you was to put you into a coma. I'm okay and now you will be too."

Todd lowered his head, kissed her lips then rang for the nurse.

For The Good Times

While out shopping on a Tuesday afternoon a few years ago, I met an acquaintance of mine, Melody Agatha Paisley, a rather colorful person, and a genuine pain in the butt as well. True to character when she thought she had an audience, Melody came bubbling over to me with an equally bubbly smile and offered her pretentious celebrity air kisses. I kept telling myself not to throw up, and just smiled as politely as possible.

Before I could say a word, she blurted loudly enough for half the world to hear, "Oh Jenny, you have to come to my holiday dinner this weekend. There's going to be a lot of people there and I want you to be one of them."

I knew this was a load of bull. The only reason I was being invited was because she knew I am transgender. Knowing I had seen her and would eventually hear about the dinner, she didn't want to risk being portrayed negatively by not inviting me. Besides, Melody just loved putting on airs and playing the "Most popular girl in town" role by filling her guest list with as many people as possible.

Deep down, I knew she wanted me there as a token to make everyone think she was open-minded and accepting of transgender people. Of course, anyone who knows her well enough, knows she is as close-minded and bigoted as one can be when it comes to the LGBT community and other minorities.

I felt bad for her husband Jack, who had voiced his dislike for the parties and the expense, while at the same time, I admired him for standing by her and supporting her. Jack was the complete opposite of Melody. He had an open mind and heart and accepted everyone equally. Jack treated everyone with the respect and dignity they deserved and received the same in return. Everyone was well aware that if it weren't for his money, Melody would have been shopping at thrift and consignment shops like so many others.

Truth be told, I dislike her dinner parties as well because, they are nothing short of boring and devoid of genuineness. Melody had a knack for inviting some of the dullest people around. When she did invite someone of interest, you couldn't get near or talk to the person because she would be draped all over them. If it was someone of high status, she would parade that person around the room like a trophy for all to see.

It was sickening if not painful to watch. I knew that I would be one of her trophies and I wasn't about to be made a fool of by her. If I was going to be made fun of, it would be on my terms. It wasn't the best attitude to have, but that was my reaction to her that day.

I was suddenly yanked back to the moment when I heard Melody saying, "See you Friday at 7." Without giving me a chance to respond, she dashed away in her whirlwind fashion. A minute or so later, I collected my thoughts and proceeded to do my shopping.

For the rest of the day, my thoughts kept getting interrupted by Melody's invitation. After a good back and forth discussion in my mind, I decided I would indeed attend her holiday dinner. I had three days to pick out an outfit and had a pretty good idea what I wanted to wear. I went to bed that night and slept peacefully.

I spent the next three days hunting down the items to complete my ensemble and when I laid them all out on the bed, I smiled with complete satisfaction. I was definitely going to be a fool on my own terms. I wasn't going to be the only one. I was filled with childlike excitement as I went into the bathroom. Stepping into the shower, I thought, "This is going to be the night of nights" and smiled.

As it turned out, luck was running with me when I arrived at Melody and Jack's house. A couple I had never seen before were entering, and I hurriedly got right behind them so I wouldn't have to make a solo appearance.

When I walked into the large living room where all the guests were seated or milling around, they all stopped what they were doing to stare at me. By the expressions on their faces, you would have thought that a demon had possessed me. I smiled widely displaying a missing tooth, having skillfully blackened it with Halloween makeup.

But that was only part of it. I was sporting jeans with the bottoms cut off and the knees ripped out, topped off with a black blouse and a copper bra on the outside that would have made Madonna jealous. The shape was made to look like metal. With hooters so pointed, I could easily have passed as the human version of the front end of a '54 Cadillac. I had capped it all off with a large, gaudy gold plastic necklace, earrings and a silver wig.

Needless to say, I was quite the sight to see. Once I let everyone have an eyeful of me, I loudly proclaimed, "Howdy, all! Where's the liquor?"

Melody rushed over to me and angrily whispered, "What do you think you're doing?"

I smiled and loudly answered, "What am I doing? I'm here to celebrate your party. Isn't that what you invited me to do?"

Melody turned to her guests who were now watching with amused interest.

"I have no idea what this person is talking about. Apparently she thinks I invited her?"

I stepped away from her and faced the group. "You know full well who I am Melody. Why you invited me in front of all those people at the market the other day.

Apparently you're the one who's mistaken."

The guests started talking amongst themselves, while some of them snickered and turned away.

Before I could say another word, or take another step, Melody grabbed me by the arm and immediately ushered me from the room, all the while stumbling for words as we moved toward the door. Jack had a smile on his face that, had Melody seen it, he would have heard about it for months afterwards.

I never received another invitation from her. In fact, I never heard from Melody again. I don't regret that fact. However, I do feel sad that because of Melody's bigotry and obsession to be the high and mighty hostess, I never got to share with those people about what it means to be transgender. It resulted in a lost opportunity to educate them about the transgender community as a whole.

Jack and I bumped into each other shortly after that night and we laughed so hard, we had tears in our eyes. He told me that Melody kept denying having known me and never once mentioned anything about my being transgender. I wasn't surprised by either statement.

As time went by, I decided to get more involved with being an advocate for the transgender community by becoming a volunteer. It was on such a day about a month ago that I was at the booth in the supermarket to raise funds for transgender youth when I heard a familiar voice say, "So this is where you've been hiding."

I looked up and saw Jack smiling down at me. Returning his smile, I said, "Yep, this is where I've been hiding."

"I think it's great that you are helping the younger transgender people. God only knows they need all the help they can get." With that, he stuffed some bills into the container.

"Thanks Jack. I really appreciate your support. Would you like a receipt for your taxes?" I asked.

He shook his head. "Do you get a break or are you chained here for the day?"

I chuckled. "I can take a break. Hold on."

"Angie," I called out to one of the other volunteers. When she turned to me I said, "I'm going to take a break. Could you cover for me?" Angie nodded and came and sat at the table.

Jack and I walked to the take-out coffee shop, got our drinks and sat at one of the cement tables in the little courtyard. Jack had coffee and I got iced tea.

"Had any more parties?" I asked after a couple moments.

Jack smiled. "As a matter of fact, Melody hasn't had one since the one you attended."

His answer surprised me. "Really?" I asked.

He nodded. "She spent the entire next day trying to convince everyone that she didn't know who you were and that she hadn't invited you. She kept trying to hammer it home that you had crashed the party."

"Hmm, I'm surprised they didn't believe her."

Jack flashed an impish grin at me.

"Okay, spill the beans. What did you do?" I smiled and took a sip of tea.

"I'm not sure, but I think I may have slipped a couple dozen times that night that Melody had indeed invited you. But, like I said, I can't be positive."

He put the coffee cup to his mouth but I could see the smile dancing in his eyes. "You are a rascal, Jack. She never found out what you did?"

Putting his cup on the table, he shook his head. "You know I honestly thought she would. Maybe even secretly hoping she would, but not one person let it out. I think that has to be a record of some sort."

I took another drink of tea. "You know I never really thanked you for continuing to be my friend so, 'Thank you'."

Jack reached over and touched my hand. "Jenny, you are my friend and, as far as I'm concerned, you always will be. You're one of the most genuine people I know and I'd take that any day over some of those plastic people that Melody brings to the house."

I looked into his eyes and saw nothing but pure sincerity in them. I could feel the tears rising in my own eyes. I finally managed to speak. "I can't begin to tell you how much that means to me. Especially, you know, with me being transgender."

Jack shook his head. "You don't get it do you?"

I didn't say anything.

"Being transgender has nothing to do with it. You're a good person, Jenny, and that's all that matters to me. When I look at you, I see a beautiful woman and a good friend."

The tears trickled down my cheeks.

Jack stood up. "Now don't go getting all mushy on me. C'mon, I'll walk you back to the store. I still have to pick up some groceries."

Jack and I see each other often and once in a while, we have lunch together and talk about everything under the sun. He's a good friend, a good man and tremendous supporter of the transgender community.

Sacred Bonds

To say that I was excited is an understatement of immense proportions. In fact, I honestly couldn't believe that I had been selected to travel with a group of scientists to Tanzania on the continent of Africa. My boss, John Sailor, editor-in-chief of the Marquis Nature Magazine, felt that I should be the one to cover the story even though I am only 22, transgender, still a novice and wet behind the ears.

The assignment seemed rather simple. I only had to chronicle the goings on of the crew, write about it and send it back to John for editing and approval. That suited me just fine since I wouldn't have to develop or create a story. It was something I could do, but preferred not to do because it was a top-notch magazine and I didn't want to risk my reputation, as new as it was, handing in a completely amateurish piece.

Equally important to me at the time, was the knowledge that, although it wasn't by choice, I was still a representative of the transgender community. As a pre-op transgender woman, I had been given an opportunity that many people could only dream about. I not only owed it to myself to be the best I could be, but I also owed it to my mom who had supported, encouraged and accepted me. She also instilled in me the belief that I could be the woman I was meant to be and have the career I always wanted. Getting to this point, however, was far from being easy.

Because I grew up in a time when being transgender was almost unheard of, I was tormented, bullied and threatened in school, to such an extent that often times I wanted to quit. I was also attacked and beaten by both boys and girls, spit on and called derogatory names.

At first, because my mother wasn't fully aware of the extent and severity of my being bullied at school, she just made phone calls to complain. However, in spite of the complaints, nothing was ever done by school officials to correct the situation. It wasn't until I came home one day with a number of physical bruises that my mother took it upon herself to put an end to the bullying.

She stormed into the Superintendent's office and demanded that he take action to stop the bullying or face a lawsuit. The fierce determination on her face and the authoritative tone of her voice got everyone's attention and no one tried to dismiss her or escort her from the office. As it turned out, she had to confront the school department many times over the course of a couple years because of the prejudicial and discriminatory behavior by the administrators towards me. It was only when my mother did hire an attorney and filed a lawsuit against the administrators and the school department that things started to change. That's when I realized the power of a mother's unconditional love. Eventually, the physical bullying stopped, but the verbal abuse continued for quite some time before it too died out.

My internal and external battles continued through high school and thankfully, began to change when I reached college. By then, I was able to begin my transitioning with the help of a gender therapist and a medical doctor who specialized in transgender hormone replacement therapy. My transitioning is still a work in progress, still filled with its ups and downs and still the happiest part of my life.

My mother's love is what gave her the courage to stand up and fight for me in every way she could. She has always been my pillar of strength. Because of her love, my dreams were being fulfilled. That being said, I was off to Africa.

We arrived at the Serengeti National Park just before sunset so I was a little disappointed with my first impression of the country. Although I knew I'd be working with professionals and scientists, I still felt a sense of anxiety and trepidation about how they were going to react to me once we were away from the United States. I was also uncertain about how African culture treated transgender people and was especially concerned about the rangers.

If the men knew of my being transgender and, I am confident they were made aware of my situation before my arrival, they never showed any signs of negativity towards me. Once all the introductions were made, my fears dissipated. We settled back while the rangers and the station attendants prepared a meal. While we were waiting to eat, we were shown to our quarters, which were basically some old army cots in a room with netting around them. To use an old movie line, "I knew I wasn't in Kansas anymore."

Oddly enough, in spite of all the excitement racing through my body, I fell asleep shortly after supper, and, if it hadn't been for one of the doctors waking me up, I would have slept the morning away. Breakfast consisted of some kind of porridge mixture, fruit and a cup of very strong coffee. I couldn't wait to get out into the wilderness to see the sights I'd heard and read so much about. Everyone at the magazine had told me the countryside was absolutely breathtaking, and I have to admit that when I stepped outside that first morning, I was in awe of the grandeur before me.

One of the park rangers came up along side me. The two of us stood looking out at nature's wonder. Without turning his head he said, 'We will be searching for a baby elephant that has been spotted alone in the deep brush about five miles from the compound."

"Do you think we will see any of the other big game animals?" I asked.

"It's difficult to say. I would best advise you don't get your hopes up."

"Why is that?"

He turned to face me. "The animals you ask about roam in a different area away from where we are going."

The news made me feel disappointed and I just nodded.

The other members of the group came out and motioned that it was time to leave so we loaded the gear into the trucks, climbed in and were off.

It didn't take long before I felt the immense heat of the African sun and wiped the sweat from my brow, thankful for the safari hat I was wearing. In spite of the advice not to get my hopes up, I couldn't help looking around, wishing I would see a lion or a water buffalo. At one point, I looked over and noticed one of the rangers smiling at me.

"What's so funny?" I asked.

He pointed to my head. "You head is like the futball," and he motioned with his head back and forth and around. Watching him made me laugh because I knew that's exactly what I must have looked like to him.

I took a small audio recorder from my pocket and began recording as we went along, which was no easy task while bouncing around and being jarred from the bumpy road. Twice, we hit some major dried up mud holes in the road and I almost lost my grip on the recorder as I grabbed the metal bar next to my head. I glanced at the rangers. They seemed unruffled by the jostling around. I quickly looked toward the scientists who, like me, were also holding on for dear life.

Before long, the trucks slowed and one of the rangers pointed to some heavy brush to the left of the truck. I couldn't see anything at first but as I kept watching, I spotted some movement and then saw the baby elephant moving about. Up until that point, my only encounter with elephants was when I had gone to the zoo or the circus or had seen them on television and in the movies. This was my first live encounter with an elephant in the wild.

I eagerly watched as the rangers jumped from the vehicles. They told the rest of us to remain in the trucks. No one spoke as the rangers coordinated their movements with hand signals. Two of them had rifles. A moment later, they raised their rifles and fired at the same time. I learned from one of the scientists that it was tranquilizer darts they had shot into the elephant before it took off running.

The rangers leaped back into the trucks and we pursued the elephant. As we rode over the rough terrain, I jammed the recorder into my pocket and held on tightly fearing I'd be jolted out of the truck. Each time the truck went airborne and violently slammed back down, we were jarred back and forth and bounced up and down. No matter how hard I clenched my jaw, my teeth banged together in my mouth so hard that I prayed they wouldn't crack. At that point, I remember I no longer envied the life of the rangers.

Ten minutes later, the elephant slowed and came to a complete halt. It staggered a bit and collapsed to the ground. The rangers and the doctors immediately ran to the animal and started working on it. One of the rangers called something over his walkie-talkie and within minutes, a large truck appeared and the elephant, now fitted with harnesses, was lifted into the back of it. With that accomplished, we proceeded to head back to the camp. Thankfully, the ride back was much more pleasant and I actually got to view the vast beauty that surrounded us.

Two days later, the baby elephant, tagged and being fed and inoculated with different shots, seemed to be settling in. During those two days, I visited the enclosure and marveled at the site of this magnificent animal. I was amazed at how such a large creature could be so vulnerable to attack and death if it wasn't properly taken care of. Even more incredible to me was how this baby, so seemingly helpless at the moment, would grow up and one day be so powerful that it would rule with majesty.

On the third morning, the baby elephant was very agitated. Before anyone could get to it to see what was wrong, an amazing thing happened. Out of the stand of trees surrounding the perimeter of the facility, came a monstrous-sized elephant with giant tusks. Not caring about anyone or anything nearby, it made its way over to the enclosure and proceeded to rip it apart with its mighty trunk and powerful legs.

Once everything was cleared, it wrapped its trunk around the chain that was securing the baby's leg to stakes and gave a super pull on it. At first, the stakes held and it looked as though the baby would be held there and the mother would fail. But then the mother slowly raised herself up on her hind legs and the stakes gave way. She moved to the baby and pushed the now loose chain from the baby's leg with her foot.

In the meantime, everyone just stood and observed. No one made an attempt to stop the mother from taking her baby, either because they felt it was best to let the two of them go, or because they were afraid of what the mother would do if they tried to interfere. The two elephants then turned and walked out of the compound with all the confidence in the world that nothing was going to stop them again.

As I watched mother and daughter disappear behind the trees, I reflected on how so much of my life I had felt trapped in a body that didn't match the way I truly felt and, like the baby elephant, may very well have remained trapped if it hadn't been for my mother rescuing me.

I was in Africa for over three weeks and saw many wonderful animals and birds and sunsets, but of all the magnificent beauty I encountered, nothing compared to witnessing the day the mother elephant broke her daughter free. It still brings tears to my eyes because it reminds me of how my mother endured all the struggles of raising me; faced all the scorn from neighbors and relatives, and stood tall and proud when she broke through the barrier of insults and hateful ridicule. In essence, she unlocked the door and set me free to experience the world around me.

Click!

After closing a divorce case in Tewksbury, Massachusetts, Cal Brent was returning home to Fall River, for some much needed rest and relaxation. What was supposed to have been an easy open-and-shut case, turned out to be a nightmare, brought on by the philandering husband's lawyer discrediting the wife. Cal was only too happy to finally be finished with the job. He was never thrilled about taking on divorce cases, but the jobs paid the bills.

A short distance from home, Cal was traveling along Bay Street in Fall River, thinking about how good a long, hot shower was going to feel. As he passed an alley, he noticed a man forcing a woman into an abandoned building. He swore under his breath because his cell phone had died and he had forgotten the charger at the office. He knew by the time he got to a phone and contacted the police, the woman could be dead and he didn't want that weighing on his conscience.

He needed to act quickly. Swerving his burgundy Mustang to the curb, he retrieved his Smith & Wesson from the glove compartment, hoping he wouldn't have to use it, yet sensing the opposite in his gut. Seventeen years as a private detective had taught him to trust his instincts.

He pulled his six-foot frame from the car and ran to the building. With gun ready in hand, he tried the door. It was unlocked. His heart started beating faster as he slowly opened the door. It was pitch black inside. Cal eased his way in and quietly pulled the door closed.

To avoid banging into something, Cal closed his eyes and waited a couple of minutes for them to adjust. When he opened them, he was able to make out a hallway to his left. Following it, he paused every few feet, to listen for any sounds. About a hundred feet along, he came to a connecting hallway. Crouching down, he cautiously gave a quick look around the corner. A short distance away, he spotted a dim light spilling into the corridor and stealthily inched his way to the door. He took a deep breath and guardedly peered into the room.

The woman was strapped to a chair with her back to him about midway in the room. Her muffled sobs reached his ears. To the left, a shadow flickered back and forth, and until Cal knew what he was up against, he was forced to remain out of sight. The woman's crying suddenly changed to anxious groans as she writhed and struggled in vain to free herself. Cal's gaze shot up to a figure standing a few feet away in front of her, smiling. The man didn't appear to have a weapon, but Cal had no choice but to remain motionless until he was certain.

"You're not too good for me now, are ya?" the man taunted the woman.

She didn't respond.

"Hey, freak, I'm talking to you," the man raised his voice.

The woman raised her head slightly. "I'm sorry. I didn't mean to hurt your feelings."

"You made a fool of me," he shot back, raising his hand as if to strike her.

She flinched. "It wasn't my fault."

"Not your fault? Not your fault? You're a damn freak. You've got a helluva nerve parading around like you're a woman, letting everyone think you're normal."

"Please, let me go," she pleaded.

"Oh, I'm gonna let you go all right. I'm gonna let you go so that you'll never make a fool out of anyone else ever again."

"Please, don't hurt me. I swear I didn't know you were interested in me. I'll move away."

He slapped the side of her head. "You made a fool of me in front of all my friends. They've been laughing at me for weeks. No, you're not getting off that easy. You're gonna pay for what you did."

At that point, Cal recognized that the voice was that of a transgender woman named Kay. She was a slender brunette who had been living in his neighborhood for a number of years and never seemed to bother anyone. That's all he really knew about her other than he thought her to be rather pretty.

Cal turned his attention back to her captive. He judged the man to be smaller than him and felt confident that, at six feet tall and much heavier, he could take the guy on if he had to. He peered back into the room.

"Please... please... let... me... go... ," Kay begged in between sobs, her head lowered again.

"You just don't get it, do you? I'm not letting you go!" her abductor snarled, throwing his hands in the air and turning his back to her. "I brought you here to rid the world of you."

While the guy still had his back to Kay, Cal seized the opportunity and rushed into the room with his gun raised. "Step back!" he commanded.

The man whirled around to see Cal's gun pointed at his chest. Still startled by Cal's sudden appearance, the man instinctively jammed his hand into his coat pocket and pulled out a pistol. Cal squeezed the trigger and the kidnapper was knocked backward, his gun clattering to the floor. He swayed then toppled over.

Cal moved further into the room and kicked the weapon out of reach. He turned to

Kay and discovered she couldn't be much younger than him. He bent down to loosen her bonds. "It's going to be…."

A maniacal laugh erupted behind Cal. Kay's wide eyes reflected the horror within. Cal spun around to see the guy pushing a button, then clearly heard a distinct click from something on the side shelf where a digital clock began counting down. Before Cal could move, an explosion knocked him off his feet and the room burst into flames.

He wasted no time shaking off the impact and rushed over to Kay. Knowing he couldn't afford to fuss with the bindings, he stooped and hoisted the chair and Kay up against his shoulder and staggered out of the room, the flames licking at his heels. In the corridor, numerous explosions hurled flames and debris in front of him, and he had all he could do to rush through them.

Between the awkward weight of Kay and the chair, and the heat and fumes sucking the air from his lungs and burning his eyes, Cal collided against the walls a number of times. Just when he thought he couldn't make it, he spotted the door and pumped his legs harder.

He slammed the chair legs into the door and stumbled out into the alley where he lost his footing and he, Kay and the chair crashed to the ground. The pressure from the jarring impact forced the air from their lungs causing both of them to groan in pain.

It took a few seconds for Cal to catch his breath. He glanced over at Kay. She was conscious and for a moment, the two just lay there staring at each other, grateful to be alive.

A few minutes passed before Cal made it to his feet. "You okay?" he finally asked Kay and set the chair on its legs.

Kay nodded. "Yeah just a little banged up, but okay." She stared up at him. "How can I ever thank you, Cal?"

"You know who I am?"

She smiled weakly. "Everyone in the neighborhood knows Cal Brent, Private Eye."

He laughed, loosened the ropes and helped her up. Just then they heard sirens blaring as the first responders raced toward the scene.

Cal suggested Kay wait in the car while he spoke to the police. Twenty minutes later, Cal and Kay were having a drink at Sandy's Tavern, a small bar in their neighborhood.

He patiently waited for the liquor to begin calming Kay's nerves before asking any questions. Because she was transgender, there was no doubt in his mind that the police were going to grill her over and over again about how she knew the victim and what had happened. He felt confident that the detectives would try to show that she was prostituting and things got out of hand when the guy found out the truth. If he could, Cal wanted to help her as much as possible and that meant uncovering every bit of information he could.

"So what's the story with this guy?" he asked rather nonchalantly.

Kay lifted the glass to her lips, took a sip, sighed and put the glass down. When she spoke, her voice was soft and still somewhat shaky. "Every so often, I go to LuchinO's on a Saturday night for some dancing and a drink. About two months ago, this guy came up to me and asked me to dance. I didn't think anything of it and accepted. We danced maybe ten or twelve times and then he left with his friends."

She took another sip of her drink. "Then, last month, I stopped in and he was there with his friends again. We said hello to each other and he asked me to dance again and then some people came in that I know and I didn't see him for the rest of the night. That was the last time I saw him until tonight."

Cal leaned back in his chair and let her words settle in his mind. As far as he could tell, she was telling the truth. He'd been to LuchinO's a few times himself and even asked a couple women to dance, so there was nothing out of the ordinary with Kay's statement.

"I take it from what I heard back there, this guy didn't know you're transgender?"

She shook her head. "I guess not. You found out the same time I did."

He leaned forward. "I don't mean to sound insensitive or offensive with this but the police are going to ask and I need to know if I'm going to be able to help you."

Kay stared at him. "Ask away."

"Are you a prostitute?"

"No," she breathed out disgustedly.

"Have you ever prostituted or said something to this guy or anyone that sounded like you were hooking?"

Kay closed her eyes, opened them again and sighed, "No."

"Not even in a kidding way?" he pressed.

Kay cleared her voice. "Not even in a kidding way."

Cal studied her face and eyes for a minute. Nothing about her demeanor or tone expressed anything but the truth in what she had answered. As he looked intently into her eyes, he noticed that behind the defensive frightened look there was a hidden beauty and found himself being drawn to it. He finished his drink and ordered another round for them.

"Look, I'm going to be honest here. I don't know much about this whole transgender stuff except for some small articles I might have glanced at or heard on television. So what made you want to be transgender? I mean, how do you know?"

Kay smiled and relaxed knowing she was with a friend.

He returned her smile and when the drinks came, Cal sat back and learned firsthand about Kay and what it meant for a person to be transgender.

She took a sip of her drink and said, "I knew when I was a kid that I was a girl."

Cal put his hand up to stop her. "Wait, wait. You knew you were transgender when you were a kid? I mean, how could you know?"

Kay smiled. "No... no I didn't know I was transgender. I just knew I was a girl. I don't know how I knew or why I knew, I just did."

"So what did you do?" Cal asked.

"At first, I didn't do anything because I didn't know what was going on. I mean

I was only a kid. I didn't understand any of it. I knew I looked like the other boys, but deep inside me, I knew I was really the same as the girls. Then one day I told my mother that I was a girl and…."

"You told your mother?" Cal interrupted her.

"Yeah I did."

"What did she say?"

"She said that I was a boy and we went back and forth for a few minutes and then she told me to go out and play. Each day for a couple weeks after that, I would get home from school and tell her I was a girl and each day we would argue about it. Finally, she told my father and he argued with me for a minute or two and then gave me a whack and said he didn't want to hear me say it again. I didn't say a word after that."

Cal leaned forward and picked up his glass to take another drink. "Damn, that had to be rough on you."

Kay took another sip of her drink and set the glass on the table. "It was rough. But the most difficult part was knowing that my parents loved me but how they couldn't really love me completely."

"What do you mean?"

"It was like they could only love the part of me they could see. They saw their son. They couldn't see me as a girl and so it made me kind of invisible and they couldn't love something they couldn't see. I know that must seem hard to understand."

"No. No, it makes perfect sense," Cal assured her. "As you were explaining it, I was trying to imagine what that would be like and I can really see how you must have felt. Yeah, that had to be really tough on you."

Kay closed her eyes for a moment reflecting on the past. When she opened them, Cal could see the tears welled up in them. "Life was not easy growing up. I had to pretend being a boy, which I hated and, even more so, hated not being able to tell anyone how I truly felt.

"Didn't anyone ever catch on or suspect that you were different?"

Kay sighed. "Yeah, sometimes someone would get an idea I was different but I made sure I learned how to fight and that pretty much squashed their suspicions."

"Have you always been this pretty?" Cal asked before he even realized what he was saying.

At first, Kay was thrown off by the question but then smiled at him in a way that made him blush.

Cal saw the twinkle in her eyes and knew the warming in his cheeks was from blushing and not from the drink. "I mean, looking at you now, no one would suspect you had been a male. What about before? Did you always look feminine?"

She smiled again while shaking her head. "No, I looked like every other boy and acted like them too. Don't get me wrong, I did have my moments with the girls as well but that's for another time."

Cal nodded. "C'mon I'll drive you home." Once she was safe inside, Cal decided to

call it a day and headed for home. He was tired. After a warm shower, he went straight to bed but sleep eluded him because all he kept thinking about was Kay's beauty and how attracted he was to her. A couple hours later, he drifted into a peaceful sleep knowing he would see her again.

It wasn't a special occasion but just another routine morning and I was looking forward to the day ahead. I was in my usual place waiting for Tom to come in for his routine morning coffee, toasted bagel and me, the "Metro News Morning Edition."

As always, at that time of the morning, the coffee shop was bustling with customers and servers and would probably appear to be a helter skelter scene for someone not used to such activity. Although, I must admit that there were plenty of moments when I thought there was no one there who knew what they were doing. Sometimes, it seemed they only got the orders straight by chance. I can say this because I had been a regular there for five years. That's when Tom first started coming into the coffee shop and placed an order for the newspaper to be there each morning with his coffee. I was the lucky one who was assigned to bring him the daily news.

Tom and I had a great relationship. He always sat inside the shop drinking his coffee, eating his bagel and perusing my pages. I made a concerted effort to always be neat, in order, and clearly printed so that he would have an easy time enjoying the read. When he finished with his meal, he would always make certain my pages were in place before neatly folding me up and carrying me under his arm to his office. In those five years, I never felt unprotected being carried to the office because he always made it a point to shield me from the wind, rain or snow. I never thought for a moment that it could be any better. Nor did I ever think my existence had real meaning. That is, until that particular morning when everything changed.

But, just a little note before I go on, because I can see some of the puzzled looks on your faces, wondering how a newspaper can be the same one day after day. It's like this, even though the news changes from day to day, the character of that particular paper is permanently embedded in the press. Each day, when the paper is printed, that character gets stamped onto the paper and carries out its duty. It's the character or personality of the paper that people get attached to and enjoy when they pick it up to read it every day. I know that seems a bit farfetched and a stretch of the imagination, but trust me, that's exactly how it is. Now that you've just learned another lesson of life, let me continue the story.

You see, Tom always placed me on his desk and, because I was in close proximity to his phone, I could hear his conversations. Well, his side of them anyway. The fact is, I learned that Tom had been born a genetic female. Yep, you read right - a female. In other words, she was… he is transgender. Did I say that right? It doesn't matter because it doesn't change the fact that Tom was once physically female, and knew deep within that she was really a male in the wrong body.

I also learned that after having a double mastectomy and taking testosterone that Tom started living his life as a male. It was a major shock to me at first, but it also gave me a greater understanding of why Tom was so gentle and kind.

On that particular morning I mentioned at the beginning of the story, Tom seemed to be in more of a hurry than usual and somewhat out of sorts about things. I say this because he really didn't spend much time reading me. My suspicions were also confirmed by the way he just quickly folded me up, without so much as taking a few seconds to straighten out my pages. Then, on the way to the office, he received a call on his cell phone and I heard him say that he believed he was going to be let go from his job because someone had complained about his being transgender. When he finished his conversation, he discarded me into one of those wire mesh trash baskets. I watched him walk away and wondered if I would ever see him again.

Not long after he had thrown me away, someone plopped a Styrofoam coffee cup on top of me and I felt the warm liquid spilling out onto the bottom of my pages. Normally, I would have been disgusted by the stains the coffee was making, but the weather was turning colder and, to be quite honest, I rather enjoyed being warmed by the coffee. The rest of the day went by without further incidence. I knew that come midnight, I would be history, which kind of saddened me because I felt my day had been wasted, and that I had been of little use to anyone. Yes, I know, I know, my character would be reborn the following morning, but it was still a somber thought to know I had served no fulfilling purpose on that day.

Resigning myself to the cold and the loneliness, I made peace with myself knowing I had done all I could to be meaningful in Tom's life. I took solace in the fact that I had presented him with some of the most interesting and informative articles on transgender rights and transgender events. Stories that I know had brought smiles to his lips and some that brought sadness and tears to his eyes. Over time, I learned about the happiness and struggle that transgender people go through and felt honored that I was the one who shared the news and stories with him. It truly was a special assignment.

I also knew that my present predicament, however sad it seemed, was not one of choice. My situation was solely caused by Tom's decision to discard me in that manner. Oddly enough, that is something I had heard from other papers about their owners. Never in a million editions had I ever thought it would happen to me.

I'm not exactly sure what time of night it was only that it had to have been before midnight when a trembling hand picked me up and carried me away. We traveled a bit of a distance on what I believed was Main Street judging by the traffic noise. I'm not certain how many turns we took, before the atmosphere changed. The traffic noise had diminished quite a bit and could be faintly heard in the distance. Wherever we were, there were no street lamps. I had no idea who had chosen to snatch me from the wire basket or why they had taken me.

We made a turn and suddenly, the openness of the street was gone, replaced by buildings on both sides. It finally came to me that we were in an alley. I knew that from the number of stories that had been printed in my pages about such places. Not only had the openness disappeared, the air changed as well. It no longer had a good smell. The alley stunk.

I didn't know whether to be relieved or frightened because most of the stories that had been printed in my pages were not good ones. From what I remembered, the alleys contained many nasty, dirty, and despicable characters. Lots of murders took place in the alleys and I didn't want to find myself ending up on a corpse. The thought of it made my pages flutter.

The person carrying me came to a stop and slowly laid out some of my pages on the ground. It was then that I recognized it was a woman who had brought me here. She undid her coat and removed two of my pages, placed them inside her clothing and wrapped them around her body. Once that was finished, she took two more sheets, wrapped them around her clothing and pulled her coat over them. She carefully folded the rest of my pages and placed them in her coat pocket.

The temperature dropped even more during the night and I could feel the woman shivering a bit in spite of the protection she had taken to warm herself. No sooner had I finished these thoughts, she raised herself up on her elbows, pulled a couple pages from her pocket, and struck a lighter to them. The fire glowed in the darkness and I could see her face, and was immensely saddened by the way she appeared and the suffering I knew she had to have endured each day.

It was strange to think that I could feel the sadness for her, yet not feel any pain from my burning pages. I noticed she had placed some small sticks on the flames, and before I knew it, she had a small fire burning. She proceeded to warm her hands and fingers. During the night, she repeated the process, pulling a couple pages from her pocket, crumpling them before putting them on the fire along with some sticks. Once the fire was burning steadily, she rested her head on her arms and warmed her hands before stuffing them inside her coat.

Morning came and the sun was shining. It was still bitterly cold, but I knew from past experiences that as the sun rose higher in the sky, it would warm up, even if only a tad. Because the woman had placed those four sheets of mine inside her clothes and coat, we both survived the night. Even with missing pages, I was jubilant because I had served a most meaningful purpose. I had helped to keep her warm and possibly aided in saving her life!

I never saw Tom again and often wondered what might have happened to him.

I still haven't been assigned another regular customer. More often than not, I get scattered here, there and everywhere and quite abused. However, I don't mind because I'm always hopeful I'll find someone who will need me in a more meaningful way.

Since that time with Tom, I have reflected on what it must be like to be transgender. The more I thought about it, the more I realized that being transgender is very similar to my own circumstances. That is, as I explained earlier, although the stories and paper itself changes, it is the imprint of the character on the paper that gives it its uniqueness. A transgender person may be born and present as one gender physically, but it is the character of the soul that truly makes them who they are.

And you thought newspapers had no life.

Flight

James Bell glided along in his vintage biplane enjoying the tremendous feeling of freedom as the ground passed below, oblivious to his presence. The force of air rushing through his hair was both exhilarating and thrilling.

He opened the throttle a little more and marveled at the raw power of the engine as it began its powerful crescendo. The small plane sped forward as though being catapulted toward the clouds, and James could feel his blood coursing through his body as his heart pumped with pure excitement. He closed his eyes and let his spirit soar with the engine's roar.

Pulsing with the steady thrumming of the plane's motor, James was in his own state of euphoria. His rapture was suddenly interrupted by a split-second sputter and then another. He yanked the throttle back, but it was too late. The motor came to an abrupt halt. He hit the starter and worked the choke to no avail. He repeated his actions over and over again, increasingly aware that he was rapidly losing altitude.

James ran through a checklist of actions he was taught to follow in aviator school and tried each one, being careful not to miss a step. The motor never made an attempt to start, so James went through the next steps, reminding himself to remain calm. Accepting the fact he would have to make an emergency landing, James peered over the side and looked for a safe place to land.

Within a short distance, he spotted a field that appeared to be long enough for him to set the plane down. All he had to do was maintain enough altitude to make it there. Judging by his rate of descent, James knew it was going to be very close. The ground sped past in what seemed like lightning speed. He held his breath and felt his entire body tense as he streamed past a stand of trees. At one point, he swore the top of a pine tree brushed the under carriage. He was afraid to look back in fearing he'd see the tail hung up in the branches.

Once cleared, he worked the rudder as he'd been taught and felt the plane level and drop in speed as he raised the nose. The wheels hit the ground with force and the small aircraft bounced up and came down and bounced again, veering to the left.

James had no control over the plane's direction and did all he could to get it down. After much fighting with the yoke, he managed to settle it down. It rolled another 30 yards before the wheel caught a rut and the nose smacked hard into the ground. James hit his head on the instrument panel and remained still for a few minutes.

When he did move, it was very slow and deliberate. He took a long, slow breath and exhaled, thankful to be alive. He let another couple minutes pass and then unhooked the harness and climbed from the plane. Moving his legs and arms left no doubt that he was bruised and would be in worse pain come the following days.

In spite of believing he had no broken bones, James moved cautiously. He made a cursory inspection of the plane. It was definitely damaged, but he believed the cost for repairs wouldn't be too bad; or at least he hoped so. Getting the plane out of the field, however, posed a whole new problem because the field, as James scanned it, was enclosed by trees. The plane was, in a sense, landlocked.

While searching for a way to rescue the airplane from its resting place, James noticed a small cabin set off in the far right corner of the field. It was barely noticeable, nestled back in amongst the pines. His spirits lifted and he set off for the house.

Upon reaching the cabin, James noticed the door was slightly ajar and cautiously approached.

"Hello," he hollered to announce his presence. "Anyone in there?" he called out while moving a little closer. "My plane's engine died on me and I had to make an emergency landing in your field."

Getting no response, he slowly approached the door and pushed it open, hoping beyond hope someone wasn't sitting there ready to blow his head off; or worse, lying dead in bed. He breathed a sigh of relief when nothing happened.

"Hello," he called again to be certain he didn't surprise or shock someone by his sudden appearance.

Again, there was no reply, so James stepped into the house and glanced around. Beneath the window to the right was a cot. In the center against the far wall stood a wood stove. A table and two chairs filled the middle of the room. There were only a few cabinets to the side of the small sink. On the other side of the room, a closet with a curtain half drawn over the opening made up the rest. He spotted a small shelf just above the sink that held 2 mugs, a plate and a pan. On top of the wood stove sat a metal coffee pot. James was surprised to see a dictionary in the middle of the kitchen table. A small basket occupied a spot to the left of the bottom cabinets and James recognized an empty can of Spam, which reminded him that he'd be able to get help through his phone.

He jammed his hand into his pocket, pulled out the phone and turned it on. He clicked to open it up and his e-mail page appeared. A crazy logo filled the screen. He closed it and hit the contact button and the phone went dead.

"Oh you stinkin'......" he started to curse just as it came on again. "Okay," he muttered and hit the contact icon. A warning flashed that he had no signal and he flared up, angry with himself for having wasted time with the logo until he realized

that it was just a leftover feed from when he had had a signal. He stuffed the phone back into his pocket.

Satisfied there was nothing in the cabin to help him out of his situation, he turned to go back to the plane and was startled when he came face to face with a grizzly old man. The guy looked like a leftover from the hippie era. His beard was shaggy and his hair was wild. James started to grin until he spotted the gun in the man's hands.

"Whoa! Now…now…now hold on there old-timer," James stammered. "My plane died and I had to land it here and…and…and I came here and the door was open. I didn't touch a thing and…and…and…I'm…I'm just trying to find out where I'm at so I can get help and get outta here."

The man motioned for James to back up which he did. "There'll be no help," the man said and motioned for James to sit.

James sat in the furthest chair trying to put some distance between him and the barrel of the gun. "If…if…it's money…" James started to say when the man put his finger to his lips letting James know to shut up.

James swallowed hard. *What the hell had he gotten himself into?* Flashes of "Deliverance" entered his mind and he shuddered.

The old man studied him. "What's your name?" he finally asked.

James cleared his throat. "It's James."

The man toyed with his beard with one hand while pointing the gun at James with the other. "James what?"

James had no idea of the significance of telling this man his last name if the guy was going to kill him anyway. But, he was in no position to protest or rebel either. "It's Bell," was all he offered.

James wasn't positive but it seemed that the old man had staggered a bit when he'd heard James' last name. Neither man spoke for at least five minutes. The silence was like a heavy veil cloaking them, making it difficult to breathe easily.

"Where you from?" the old man seemingly choked the words out.

James studied him while debating whether to tell the truth or not. He opted for the truth. "Originally from Rehoboth, Mass, but now I live in Little Compton, R.I."

If James didn't know better, he'd have sworn the guy was shot by the way he reeled back when he heard the information. He wondered what could possibly cause such a reaction.

The man pulled the other chair away from the table and sat down. He glanced up towards the ceiling then back at James. He nodded his head a bit then said, "Your mother's name Delia?"

It was James' turn to look stunned. "Yes. Yes it is," he replied, studying the man even more intently than before. "Who are you? Do I know you?" James asked, hoping not to anger the guy.

"What's your father's name?" the old man asked, ignoring James' question.

Still trying to figure out who the old man was and what was going on, James replied, "It's Paul. Paul Bell. Now who the hell are you?"

The old man cleared his throat. "The name's Martin. Martin Macomber."

Not recognizing the name at first, James dismissed it. But after mulling it over for a few minutes, the name registered in his mind. "Macomber, you're the guy who broke into our house and tried to hurt my mother."

The old man's nostrils flared and he stood up, pointing the barrel of the gun at James. "I did no such damn thing."

"My father told……."

"Your father was a no-good-for-nothing-hood. He made that story up."

"He didn't make it up," James shot back at him.

"Your father was a liar, a cheat and a two-bit hood that used his connections to get me out of the picture."

"You broke into our house. My mother identified you," James snarled.

Martin shook his head. "You damn fool kid. What the hell do you know?"

"Then you tell me," James spat.

"I never broke in that night. I was there because your mother let me in."

James started to protest, but Martin silenced him with a wave of the gun.

"You wanted to hear my story, well shut up and listen."

"Your mother and I were sweethearts before your father moved into town. He took a liking to her immediately and with his fancy cars and money he was able to lure her away from me. Shortly after she married him, she told me she had regretted it."

"What are you talking about?" James challenged. "If she didn't love him, why did she stay with him?"

Martin chuckled. "She was afraid of him, that's why. But we were planning on running away and somehow, your father got wind of it. So the night I was there making arrangements with your mother, your father came home early. We had already concocted a story that if that ever happened she was to tell him I broke in so he wouldn't hurt her."

James sat up in the chair. "I don't believe it." As he spoke the words, fragments of memories invaded his thoughts. Memories that seemed to verify what Martin was saying. He leaned forward and rested his arms on the table. "No, no, I… I don't believe it. She would never cheat on my father."

"Don't you dare sully your mother's name like that," Martin snarled. "We weren't having an affair. Yes, we still loved each other, but in order to be together, she had to divorce him. Naturally, with his powerful friends, we knew the only way she could do it was to get away from him first."

James sat back in the chair. "I still don't think she'd do something like that."

Martin then backed up to the window above the bed where he removed something from the windowsill behind the curtain. He moved to the table and sat down. Watching James the whole time, he placed a small picture frame face down on the table and slid it over to James.

James leaned forward and flipped the frame over. Looking up at him was a picture of his mother when she was younger and a picture of a man, who could very easily

have been a young Martin.

He slid the picture back toward Martin. "This could have been anyone. It doesn't prove a thing," James said, knowing his words sounded hollow and weak.

Martin smirked. "No, I suppose to a snot-nosed kid like you it wouldn't."

"I'm not a kid, in case you haven't noticed."

"You're a kid to me. Listening to you I could throw up. You sound just like your father; a know-it-all. Afraid to face the truth even when it smacks you right in the mouth."

"I'm not my father. I'm nothing like him. You think I'm a know-it-all. Well, buddy, you had better take another look in the mirror because you don't know squat about me."

Martin squinted, letting a few minutes pass before speaking again. "I'll tell you what I do know. You're a damn liar."

James stared at him. "I'm not lying about anything," he said loudly while trying not to shout.

"You're still lying," Martin shot back.

James threw his hands up in the air. "Okay, so what am I supposed to be lying about?"

"What are you lying about?" Martin repeated. "Delia never had a son named James. She had a daughter. Janice was her name if I'm correct. So what do you have to say now?"

"You're right. My mother did have a daughter Janice. I was Janice."

Martin laughed. "You expect me to believe that cock and bull story?"

"It's true," James said in a calmer voice.

Martin squinted. *This guy must think I'm an idiot. What's his game?* When he spoke again, his voice was dripping with sarcasm. "What did you do? Did you trade your body in at the body shop for a new one?"

James slapped the table. "I'm transgender, you old fool."

Martin shook his head. "Don't give me that crap."

"What have you been doing all these years? Have you been living under a rock?"

"Shut up," Martin snarled. *This was getting crazier by the minute. Where the hell did this guy come from?* He had to focus. He got up from the chair and backed up to the door and peered out toward the plane, then glanced back at James. "So how did you find me? Did your old man send you to look for me?"

James cleared his throat. "First of all, I didn't find you. I crashed landed in your field as you can see. Secondly, my father didn't send me."

"And I'm supposed to believe that?"

James stared hard into Martin's eyes. "My father's dead. Been dead for over three years now, so if you still think he sent me, then you've got mental problems."

Martin smirked. *If anyone has mental problems it's you pal.* He brushed the thought aside and continued to stare at James. There was something about the conviction in James' voice that told Martin he was telling the truth. In spite of his thoughts, he pushed James anyway. "He's dead?"

James shook his head. "Yeah, he's dead. If you want proof, I've got news for you. I don't carry his death certificate in my pocket."

Martin chuckled but didn't say anything. When he did speak, it was much quieter. "So you come looking for me on your own then?"

Again, James shook his head in disbelief. "I didn't come looking for you. No one is looking for you. I never heard my father say he was looking for you. The only thing I heard him say about you was, 'good riddance'. That was it. You want to believe me, fine. If you don't, that's fine too. Do what you have to do."

Even though James' defiance riled him up because it reminded him of James' father Paul, Martin couldn't help but like James. Something inside of him said that James was a man of integrity and good character. "Your old man must have loved having the son he always wanted."

James lowered his head. When he raised it again, there was sadness in his eyes. "Not really. To him I was just a freak. A freak he disowned. After all, he couldn't have his daughter showing up in men's clothes. What would all his friends and associates think? He gave me a choice in no uncertain terms. If I wanted to remain in his house and enjoy that lifestyle, I would have to do so as his daughter. Otherwise, I would have to disappear on my own without help from him or anyone else. Nice, huh?"

Silence filled the room once again, but this time it was not suffocating. Martin looked at the window above the bed. *What the hell would I do if I had a kid who wanted to be a boy? Would I think she, he was a freak?*

James broke the silence. "So, is it true what happened between you and my mother?" he asked, his voice soft and questioning.

Martin only glanced at James before lowering his head. He closed his eyes, inhaled deeply, lifted his head and nodded. "Yes."

James watched as Martin gently lowered the gun, sat down and stared at the wall above James' head. A moment later, Martin's eyes filled with sadness as his shoulders slumped.

To witness this man wilt before him, James was moved. In his heart he now knew what Martin had told him was the closest thing to the truth. He gently cleared his throat and said, "Martin, I believe you."

When Martin lifted his head, James continued, "I'm not here to get you. I am not your enemy. He's dead."

Martin swallowed hard and nodded. "I can't offer you anything to eat. I ran out of money last week and don't have any food."

Money, that's what had been quietly nagging James. How had Martin survived?

James stared at Martin for a long moment. Then it came to him. He remembered his father and mother arguing about money being stolen. James tried hard to recall the amount. He just had to be patient and it would come.

"I have a couple chocolate bars in the plane."

Martin nodded. "That's good enough for me."

James cautiously stood up, nodded and headed for the plane. He retrieved the candy bars and walked slowly back to the house. Halfway there, the amount of 25 thousand dollars popped into his mind. His mother had suffered much because of that money. The more James thought about his mother suffering, the more his anger welled up inside him.

When he entered the house, Martin was at the sink. The gun was resting on the table. James snatched it up and pointed it at Martin's back. "You caused my mother to suffer," he snarled and moved his finger to the trigger.

Martin glanced over his shoulder and was shocked to see James holding the gun. He dropped the coffee pot into the sick and spun around.

"What the hell is this?"

"What does it look like?"

Martin shook his head. "So, this was all a ruse to get me to let my guard down so you could haul me in to your father."

"I told you my father's dead, but not before he put my mother through hell for the 25 grand you stole."

Martin put his hands up. "Hold on there. I didn't steal a damn thing. I don't know……"

James lifted the gun a little higher. "Shut up. I'm not falling for it. You fooled me once. I'm not buying your bull anymore."

Martin's anger filled his eyes. "You snot-nosed kid, you don't know a damned thing. If I wasn't telling the truth, why didn't I shoot you? Why are you the one now holding the gun?"

Visions of his mother being beaten by his father flashed through James' mind. Rage filled him and he felt his finger tighten on the trigger.

"My mother suffered because of you."

"I'm telling you……"

"Telling me what?" James snarled. "Telling me you're innocent? That you didn't know anything about the money? I don't want to hear it. Now I'm telling you how it's going to be."

Martin glared at him. There was nothing he could do while James held the gun pointed at him. Inside, he was raging. He wasn't angry at James but at himself for having been so careless. He should have known better.

Martin shook his head and smiled. "You're wondering how I made it all these years, aren't you."

"As a matter of fact I was trying to figure that out."

"So you just automatically assumed I stole it."

James nodded. "That's right. You mentioned about going for groceries, which means you must have a car or truck or something. Where is it?"

Martin defiantly stared at him.

James waved the gun. "It doesn't matter to me. I'll just tie you up and go look for it myself. It's up to you."

The look in James' eyes showed he meant business so Martin tilted his head toward the back of the shack. "It's out back through the woods about 25 yards."

James backed up toward the door. "Let's go."

Martin sighed and headed for the door.

Outside, James stepped far enough away to let Martin lead the way.

The truck was where Martin had claimed it would be and James quickly noticed how the green of the truck blended it with its surroundings, shielding it from passersby.

James watched Martin closely as they got into the truck, making sure to keep the gun pointed, but at a position where Martin couldn't snatch it from his hands. He kept his finger on the trigger.

Martin was wise enough to know that to make a grab for the gun would be a fool's move. He'd stayed alive all these years and wasn't about to get his head blown off acting stupidly.

"Where's the nearest town?" James asked.

"Collett, about five miles from here," Martin answered calmly.

The men drove in silence as Martin steered the truck along the winding country road. When they reached Collett, James spotted a public telephone. "They still have telephone booths here?"

Martin glanced at the booth ahead. "Yep," was all he said.

"Does it work?"

Martin pulled over and parked the truck. "It did a couple weeks ago."

James looked down at the gun, knowing he couldn't take it outside. "C'mon, get out and go over by the phone where I can keep an eye on you."

Without arguing, Martin eased himself from the truck and walked over to the telephone.

James left the gun in the truck and proceeded to the phone and dropped some change into it, then dialed a number. "Hello," he said after a moment. "What's that? No, operator I don't have any more change. Well, can you put this through as a collect call? You can? That's great. Yes, it's from James, James Bell. Thank you, operator."

After a number of rings, James said, "Thank you. Oh, operator can you try one more number for me? Okay it's…hold on a moment please. I have to get the number from my wallet."

James took his wallet out and searched for the small paper with his uncle's number. They didn't bother with each other too much, but the old man had told James if he ever needed him, to call. With the number in hand, James looked up and noticed Martin was gone.

He cussed for having been so distracted. Why he ever thought Martin would just stay there was totally stupid. James gave the operator the number and listened while she explained to his uncle that it was a collect call and waited. He looked around for Martin knowing he should go looking for him. Just then, his uncle's gruff voice came through the phone.

"Hello."

"Uncle Charles, it's James and….."

"I know who the hell it is. The operator just told me. You think I'm stupid?"

"No. No I don't think you're stupid, I just said it that's all. I need a favor."

"What is it? You need money?"

"No, I don't need any money."

"Then why the hell you callin' collect? I'm not stupid. I'm old, but I'm not stupid."

"I'm at a pay phone and ran out of change."

"A pay phone!" Uncle Charles interrupted. "They don't have pay phones anymore. You think I'm stupid? Where's your celibate phone or whatever the hell ya call it?"

"It's a cell phone," James heard himself yelling back. He lowered his voice. "Please, just listen a moment. I need you to go to Dan's house and tell him to come pick me up. I'm in…" he paused realizing he didn't know where he was. "Hold on a moment, Uncle Charles."

"Don't take all damn day. I'm payin' for this call. You think I forgot? You think I'm stupid?"

James spotted a woman coming out of the small convenience store. "Excuse me," he asked politely. "Could you tell me the name of this town? I broke down and I'm trying to get my family to come pick me up." He pointed to the receiver in his hand as proof.

"You're in Collett," she answered. Then seeing the puzzled look on his face, continued saying, "Collett, Connecticut."

James smiled. "Thank you. I appreciate your help."

He turned his attention back to the phone. "Uncles Charles, it's Collett, Connecticut." Not getting any response, James spoke much louder into the receiver. "Uncle Charles, are you listening to me?"

James heard a snort and then his Uncle said, "Who is it?"

"Uncle Charles, it's James. Tell Dan to come get me in Collett, Connecticut. Can you remember that or do you want me to wait till you get a paper and pencil?"

"Don't get smart with me James or I'll clip you upside the head when I see you. I know what you said. You think I'm stupid?"

"Could you please repeat the name for me?" James asked his voice softer to calm his uncle down before the conversation got totally lost.

"What do I gotta repeat it for? This is costin' me money. You think I forgot? You think I'm stupid?"

James had all he could do to keep his temper. He remained silent.

"It's Collett, Connecticut. I know where that is, you know. You think I don't know? You think I'm stupid?"

Out of respect for his uncle, James remained silent, all the while thinking to himself that he was the stupid one for having called his uncle in the first place. As soon as he was calm enough, he said, "Thank you, Uncle Charles. I appreciate you doing this for me. I'll give you the money for the phone bill when I get home."

"You better give it to me. And don't make me wait for it either or I'll have a good mind to vig you for it."

James hung up the phone and walked back to the truck. The gun was where he had left it but the keys were not in the ignition. Another mistake he'd made. He shook his head and closed the door. His stomach gurgled in protest. He was hungry. Figuring he had time, he looked around and spotted a diner not too far from the truck and headed for it.

Almost two hours and three cups of coffee later, James glanced up in time to see Dan come walking into the diner.

"Kind of figured when I rolled into town and looked around that you'd be here," Dan said cheerfully.

"You want a coffee or something to eat?" James offered before he stood up.

"I'm all set," Dan replied.

James left some bills on the table and they left the restaurant. Looking to his left, James noticed the green truck was gone. "So the old guy doubled back," he said softly.

"What's that?" Dan asked.

"I'll fill you in on the way," James replied and they got into Dan's truck and headed for home.

When James finished, Dan smiled. "So the old guy's been hiding out ever since then? What do you think he'll do?"

James looked out the side window, and then turned to Dan. "He'll probably rabbit like he did before. He knows I'll be coming back for the plane so he won't go back to the house."

"You gonna go looking for him?"

"What for? I don't have anything against the guy. Besides, that was my father's stupid way of doing things, not mine."

When they reached home, James said, "Do me a favor and drop me off at my uncle's house so I can give him the money for the phone before he decides to vig me?"

Dan laughed. "Your uncle's going to charge you interest?"

James chuckled. "Yeah, he threatened to vig me if I didn't pay for the phone bill right away."

Dan laughed again. "I know it's not your lifestyle, but you have to admit, your family had some colorful characters in it."

James looked at him. "Colorful is not a word I would use to describe them. You're lucky you didn't have to grow up with that crap."

At first, Dan smiled because the truth of the matter was he did know all the crap James and his mother had gone through. Dan had had a secret crush on Janice for many years. When Janice told him she was really a boy, Dan was heartbroken. But feeling so deeply, Dan supported her and they became the best of friends. That devotion never wavered. Deep down, Dan still had feelings that he kept buried. "Actually I do know….."

"Stop," James interrupted. The tone of James' voice let Dan know to let the subject drop.

"You want me to wait for you?"

"No, I'm going to stop in at my mother's house and then I'll walk home."

"That's over two miles."

"I need to get my frustrations out."

Dan dropped James off at his uncle's house. "If you change your mind call me."

James rang the doorbell and waited. Two minutes later, his uncle opened the door. Uncle Charles stared at him. "Whatta ya doin' here? You told me you were in Colorado."

"I was in Connecticut," James corrected him. "Don't you remember?"

"You think I don't remember? You think I'm stupid? Connecticut, Colorado, I know the difference you know. You think I don't? You think I'm stupid?"

"Uncle Charles, I don't think you're stupid. I know you know the difference. I came to give you the money for the collect call I made to you earlier."

Uncle Charles nodded. "Yeah, I remember that call. I'm not stupid. What were you doin' in Colorado anyway?"

James opened his mouth to correct him, thought better of it and said, "I had business to take care of."

"I thought you didn't want anything to do with the family business?" Uncle Charles asked, at the same time scanning the yard to be sure they were alone.

"It was personal business, not family," James said hoping that would put an end to the questioning.

"Smart answer," Uncle Charles replied. "I like that." He pointed a finger at James. "You're gonna do good for the family. I know when someone's got what it takes. I'm not stupid you know."

James removed a twenty dollar bill from his wallet and handed it to Uncle Charles.

"What's this? You givin'me a payoff?" Uncles Charles said without taking the money. "I'm not stupid you know. I know what a payoff is. You settin' me up James? I know what a setup is. I'm not stupid you know."

James shoved the money into Uncle Charles' hand. "It's not a payoff. It's for the damn phone bill for the call I made this morning."

In a quick movement that caught James by surprise, Uncle Charles gave him a swat on the side of the head. "Get smart with me and I'll take you downstairs and teach you a lesson. You think I can't do it? You think I'm stupid? Try me."

James just shook his head and turned to leave. Then looking back at Uncle Charles he said, "I'm going to see my mother and then I'm going home."

Uncle Charles looked at the money in his hand. "This better cover the call from Colorado, cuz if it's not, I'll vig you for tryin' to stiff me. I'm not stupid you know."

"It's enough," James called over his shoulder and kept walking.

Just as James rounded a curve in the road, he spotted Martin's truck coming from his mother's driveway and started running.

Martin caught sight of James running towards him and jammed his foot on the accelerator. The truck jumped forward sending gravel and dirt shooting out the back. His heart was beating fast and hard. The last thing he expected was to see James bounding toward him. He checked his rearview mirror and felt a little relief when he didn't see James. He had to think fast and plan on getting away from the area as fast as he could without drawing attention.

James didn't waste time chasing Martin any further. It was more compelling to check on his mother. He dashed into the house and seeing the startled look on his mother's face, he knew she was all right. He spun around and ran out the door, his mother's voice calling after him. James ran to the garage and jumped into his Jeep. He immediately called Dan.

"Meet me at the field," was all he ordered as he sped out of the driveway.

When he reached the field where he kept his other plane, he spotted Dan waiting for him. "Help me get her ready for takeoff," he yelled from the Jeep.

Dan didn't question and immediately hurried to release the cables holding the plane to the ground stakes. James unhooked the other side and was climbing into the plane when he noticed Dan staring at him.

"That... that s.o.b. was at my mother's house. I'm going to find out where he is."

Dan held his hand up. "What good's it going to do you?"

James waved him off. "What are you talking about?"

"You need someone on the ground. You spot him from the sky, you let me know, and I can track him from the ground. He won't be expecting you to be in the sky or me coming after him."

"It'll take too long," James objected.

"What are you going to do if you do find him? You going to ask him to wait while you find a parking space for the plane?"

James swore under his breath. In his anger he hadn't thought about the plane once he found Martin. He glanced down at Dan. "Okay. I'll circle till I locate him and let you know where he is."

"Now you're talking," Dan replied and headed for his truck.

James started the plane, checked all his instruments and then rolled the plane from the barn he'd transformed into a hangar. He taxied to the small runway in the field behind the building. A moment later, the plane lifted into the sky and headed in the direction he last saw Martin going. He knew Martin would try to use every skill he had to evade being spotted. James hoped Martin wouldn't expect to be seen from the air. Fifteen minutes later, he spotted Martin's green truck traveling on the back roads through Little Compton heading for Westport, Massachusetts in the complete opposite direction he would take if he were returning to Connecticut.

James put his headset on and turned on the phone's bluetooth. Within seconds, he was in touch with Dan. "He's headed toward Westport, moving toward East Road."

"Gotcha," Dan answered. "I'm on my way. Do you think he'll stay on that route?"

"My guess is," James said into the mouthpiece, "that he'll try to get to the highway. He's got to be familiar with all the roads around here so I don't expect him to stay in a straight line."

After five minutes, James spoke up. "That sly little bugger."

"What's he doing?" Dan's voice piped through the earpiece.

"He made a U-turn and is heading back to you."

"I'm on East Road now, just past the Maiden Equestrian Farm, so how much distance between us?" Dan asked.

"You're about three… hold on… he's turning again. I know what he's doing. Good move."

"What's a good move? Where is he?" Dan said, frustrated James wasn't filling him in.

"I know where he's going," James responded.

"Would it be too much to fill me in so I know where I'm going?" Dan pressed.

"Sorry," James apologized. Feeling a little more relaxed now that he believed he knew what Martin was doing. "He's zigzagging, heading for Crandall Road."

"Crandall Road?" Dan questioned. "Why go there?"

"He's going to head straight out to Stafford Road and then onto the highway and back to Connecticut," James answered with strength and confidence in his voice. "Don't bother following him now. I want you to head for the Stafford Road Junction. I'll stay with him from up here."

Hearing the conviction in James' voice, Dan simply said, "Done."

James followed Martin without a problem. That is, until Martin pulled to the side of the road and went into the woods. When Martin reappeared, he looked up at the circling plane, waited a moment then jumped into his truck.

Martin waited a few minutes before starting the engine. He kept glancing out his windshield and side window to note the plane's passing. After observing it passing overhead three times, he started the engine, shifted into gear and made a U-turn.

"What the heck?" James said aloud.

"What's wrong?" Dan immediately asked.

"He's doubling back again," James said, a touch of puzzlement in his tone.

"You want me to head back?" Dan asked, easing his foot off the gas to let the truck slow down.

"No," James replied. "You get to Stafford Road. I'll stay with him. I know he's going to head your way again."

"Gotcha," was all Dan said and stepped on the pedal again.

Martin could hear the steady whine of the plane's engine and knew it had to be James following him. He had sensed being followed earlier, but dismissed it until he went into the woods and watched the plane circling. He was sure of it now and had to decide what to do. Moments later, he knew exactly what plan of action he should take and pressed the gas pedal almost to the floor. He smiled as the old truck picked up speed.

James was making another pass when he spotted Martin's truck taking a turn that went against everything James had calculated Martin would do. He watched with puzzling curiosity while trying to figure out what the old man was up to.

After watching the truck take various turns, James began thinking that maybe Martin was confused and thought he had been going in the wrong direction and was now trying to find his way again. Not once, did James anticipate Martin's next move.

Martin reached the main road but, instead of going right, which would take him to Tiverton and home, he swung the truck left heading back to Little Compton.

Confused by Martin's erratic movements, James scratched his head and said, "What are you up to, old man?"

Dan's voice came through the headset. "What's he doing?"

"He's heading back to Little Compton."

"Why would he do that?" Dan asked, his voice reflecting the same confused puzzlement as James.

"Beats the hell out of me," James said, attempting to recalculate Martin's intentions. "Damn," he cursed seconds later.

"What happened?"

"He's heading for my mother's house," James barked into the mouthpiece.

"I'm on my way," Dan replied and swung the truck around as soon as he could.

James pushed the throttle, knowing that even with the increased speed he wouldn't make it to the house before Martin. He swore, realizing he had underestimated the old man. He figured it must have been when Martin had gone into the woods and emerged that he had been spotted. James knew he should have formed a wider circle to keep from being so obvious. He shook his head, letting go of the regrets, and turned his attention back to the moment. He had to be completely focused so as not to make another mistake.

James watched with a sickening feeling in his stomach as Martin's truck sped into his mother's driveway. As he passed overhead, James spotted Martin running toward the house carrying the gun. He cursed again for having been so arrogantly confident that he had figured the old man out.

The plane hadn't completely stopped moving when James climbed from the cockpit onto the wing and jumped to the ground. He rolled a couple times and was up and making a mad dash for the house, hoping he would be in time to save his mother.

When he was close enough, James found shelter behind the hedges and made his way to the front of the house, guessing that it would be the last place Martin would expect him to enter. He edged his way to the front door, took a deep breath and slowly opened it. He listened a moment then pushed the door open enough to slip inside.

Martin was nowhere to be seen. James listened for voices but didn't hear any and wondered, if while he was landing the plane, Martin had killed his mother and then committed suicide. The gruesome thought made him shiver. In spite of wanting to dash from room to room, James stealthily made his way toward the kitchen located in the back of the house. Not seeing anyone, he moved inside the room to look out the back window, thinking Martin may have escaped that way.

James looked out the window, scanning the perimeter for signs of a fleeing

Martin, but didn't spot him at all. He turned and froze at the sight of Martin aiming the gun at his chest. Even though he was terrified that Martin would pull the trigger, James marveled at the way the old man was able to move about so quietly.

"Where's my mother?" James asked, finding his voice again.

Martin sneered at him. "So you weren't looking for me, huh?"

"I wasn't until I saw you here."

"You're a liar," Martin said, his voice spewing venom.

"Look I know how…"

"You don't know anything," Martin spat. "You're just like your old man. You can't be trusted."

"And you can by coming back here with a gun?" James challenged. "Now where's my mother?"

Martin knew that as long as he kept his mouth shut, he'd have a better chance at staying alive. "You'll know when I'm ready to let you know," was all he offered.

James took a step forward.

Martin lifted the rifle up to his shoulder, his finger moving to the trigger. "Don't be too hasty. I'll kill you if I have to. Now step back."

James did as he was told, not wanting to risk calling Martin's bluff. He took a step back and leaned against the counter. "You've got no way out of here you know."

Martin stared at him for a long moment, realizing that what James had said was true. Sure there were roads he could take to get out of the area but he would be easily caught. The only thing he could do would be to tie James up in the hopes of having enough time to flee the area.

Dan parked his truck at the beginning of the driveway. Not knowing what was going on inside, he cautiously made his way toward the house. The front door was slightly ajar. Unsure of what he would be walking into, his heart beat faster. He took a deep breath and eased inside. The living room was empty. He breathed a sigh of relief and tried to lick his lips, but his mouth was dry from nerves.

Listening carefully, he heard the sound of muffled voices coming from the kitchen. While inching his way slowly in that direction, Dan tried to assess what was going on. When he was close enough, he looked quickly into the room and saw Martin holding the gun on James.

Just then, Martin noticed James' eyes widen and before he could move to see the cause, he was grabbed from behind.

Dan lunged at Martin and wrestled the gun from his hands. He knocked Martin to the floor.

James was by his side in a flash. "Where's my mother?" he demanded.

"I'm right here," a soft voice came from behind them.

James turned to see his mother standing in the doorway holding a bag. "What's going on?" she asked without knowing Martin was on the floor.

James and Dan turned sideways to allow Delia Bell a chance to see Martin's sprawled body.

She dropped the bag on the floor, tomatoes and other vegetables spilling out. "What have you done to him?" she said, pushing both James and Dan aside so she could get to Martin.

"What have we done to him?" James replied. "He came here to kill you, that's what he's done."

She stood and looked up into James' bewildered eyes. "He did no such thing, you damn fool."

"He had a gun," Dan offered, holding the gun out so she could see.

"Well he doesn't have it now, does he?"

She turned back to James. "Are you going to be like your father?"

Still stunned by her reaction, James stood with his mouth open. Finally he said, "He stole the money from Dad and I……"

"You what?" she questioned. "You went after him taking up where your father left off?"

"No, it wasn't like that," James defended himself. "I'm not my father."

"Then help him off the floor," she commanded and watched as the two men lifted Martin to his feet.

"I'm so sorry, Martin," she apologized.

James and Dan looked at each other totally taken aback.

"All of you, sit down at the table and behave," she ordered and proceeded to pick the vegetables up off the floor.

The three men sheepishly made their way to the dining room table and sat down, none of them saying a word, but all looking like misbehaving school kids who were now being admonished.

When Delia had the coffee and pastry on the table, she sat down. "Now tell me what's going on."

James told her everything from his emergency landing right up to the moment she came into the room.

Delia listened attentively and when he finished she said, "Martin never stole any money. Money was stolen. Yes. But it wasn't Martin who stole it. I did."

"You?" James started to protest, but she waved him off.

"Yes, I stole it. But before I explain that, I think the three of you need to take a sip of your coffee while I put things into perspective. I don't want any interruptions. Wait until I'm finished before you make any remarks."

Puzzled, the three men looked at each other, took a sip of coffee and waited for Delia to continue.

Delia took a mouthful of her own coffee, pursed her lips and exhaled slowly. When she spoke, her voice was soft as though it was coming from some far away place in the past. "Martin and I were sweethearts until Paul, your father, moved into town. At first, I ignored his advances, but over time, I found him to be attractive and a good man. I had no idea how he was slowly manipulating things to push Martin out of the picture. It wasn't until after we were married that I learned the truth about him

and his business.

"Shortly after our marriage began, I learned that I was pregnant, which dashed my hopes of breaking away from Paul. Paul wasn't stupid and he was highly suspicious of everything he couldn't or didn't understand. He was suspicious about the baby being his, but because there was no specific time period of exactly when I got pregnant, he let it go…or so I thought. When I went for my checkup, the doctor made me swear in total confidence that I would never let on what he had to tell me. He said that your father had offered him a thousand dollars to tell him whether or not the baby was his. When the doctor said it was, your father continued offering more money up to five thousand dollars.

"The doctor assured him that you were his child but your father just couldn't let it go. That's when he started physically beating me and mentally abusing me. He swore he would kill me if I ever stepped out of line. I believed him and so I stayed and put up with it. Martin and I continued to see each other, but we were always afraid someone would see us or worse, would tell your father. Because of the way things were, Martin and I avoided being intimate with each other.

"Finally, when you were a little older James, I had had enough. I decided to leave your father because I was sick and tired of the way he bullied and abused me. Everything was about money with him and it was the only way I knew I could hurt him. The night Martin and I planned to run away, your father came home and almost caught us. That money was to help us start a new life.

"Instead, because I couldn't get away after that, I sent the money to Martin to live on. Because your father was so brutal, Martin couldn't get any good respectable jobs and the money ran out fast. Your father started to become suspicious of me and I had to stop sending the money. After that, I lost touch with Martin and thought I'd never see him again."

James looked at Martin and shook his head realizing how wrong he had been. He knew that he, of all people, shouldn't have jumped to conclusions. Being transgender, James learned early what it was like to be discriminated against, and he knew how wrong it was to judge someone falsely. That was something that had happened to him over and over again. He now understood why Martin had acted as he had. He stuck his hand out. "I'm sorry."

Martin stared at him a moment before saying anything. He nodded. "Thank you for saying that. It means a lot to me." He shook James's hand. "So you were Delia's little girl, huh?"

"I was," James replied. "Well, physically anyway."

Martin kneaded his chin. "What made you want to become a man?"

"Long story short," James said, "In my heart I always knew I should have been a male. I don't know how I knew, I just did. Growing up, I tried everything I could to shake the feelings off, but instead of going away, they just got stronger and stronger and I knew they were real and wouldn't go away until I did something about it. As you can see, I did just that."

Martin leaned his elbows on the table. "It's true then, you're not after me?"

James nodded. "It's true, Martin."

Delia cleared her throat. "There's another piece of the puzzle that I need to clear up while we are all here putting the cards on the table so to speak."

The three men looked over at her and waited.

"The truth of the matter is…the truth of the matter is that Martin is your real father James."

Martin and James looked stunned. Dan sat back in his chair and whistled.

"Yes, Martin," Delia continued. "Janice was your daughter, who is now James, your son."

Martin buried his face in his hands. All the unanswered questions he had earlier about what he would do if he had a transgender child were answered in that moment. When he looked up, tears were trickling down his cheeks. "I don't know what to say. All those years I wasted, moving from one place to another thinking my life was in danger. Then living in that cabin alone in fear of showing myself and scratching out a living doing menial jobs." He shook his head. "You have no idea what that was like and now you tell me it's finished and that I have a son."

James looked at Martin. "We've got a lot of catching up to do if you feel it's something you want to do."

Martin looked from one face to another. "Is it really over?"

Delia got up and went over and embraced him, tears streaming from her own eyes. "It's over Martin. It's really over."

Amazonian Secret

Although it did happen, I'm still finding it hard to believe and I'm not even sure where to begin. I guess the best place to start is right at the beginning. It was almost a year ago to the day that I had an experience that changed my life and will continue to have its effects on me for the rest of my life.

It was June 24 and nothing special was happening that day so I thought I would drive down to the beach and relax in the morning sun before it got too hot. With sunscreen and a book in hand, I headed out the door, glad to be getting away from the city. Because it was a weekday and after the morning rush, driving was relatively easy and quite relaxing.

When I arrived at the beach, I was thrilled to see only one other car parked alongside the road and I parked right behind it. A big smile appeared on my face brought about by the smooth way things were flowing along. That was about to change.

The owner of the other car was quite a ways down the shoreline and I could see a fishing rod sticking up out of the sand. I knew I'd have the beach to myself unless others arrived, which wasn't too often because not a many people knew the beach was there.

I laid out my beach towel and unfolded the beach chair. Because I am transgender and on hormones, I take extra precaution against skin cancer and slather on the sunscreen. Just as I started to unbutton my blouse, I felt something brush against my foot. My surprise turned to horror when I looked down and saw a toadstool sticking out from between my toes. As I stared at my foot in utter disbelief, something began moving beneath my skin. My first instinct was to knock the toadstool off my foot but I was terrified as I watched a toad appear and slowly climb up the toadstool and perch itself on top.

Once I got over the initial shock, I tried shaking it all away, but no matter how hard I tried, they didn't budge. I dropped into the beach chair and lifted my foot to remove them but when I went to grab the toad, it dashed off and somehow slipped back into my foot. I yanked on the toadstool, but that only caused a lot of pain and when I held my foot up to examine it, I was stunned to see the toadstool was growing out from between my toes.

Bewildered and shaken up, it took a few moments before I regained my composure and started to take action. Hurriedly, I packed everything up, ran to the car and threw everything inside. At the same time, I frantically searched for my cell phone so I could call my doctor. The longer it took to find the phone, the more discombobulated I became, which only made me fumble around all the more. At that point, there was no such thing as remaining calm.

During the time I groped for the phone, I refused to look at my foot for fear that I would see it was still sprouting that grotesque toadstool. Another reason I didn't want to see it was because the mere thought of it was making my stomach queasy and I couldn't afford to be sick at that moment. While shaking my purse around, I couldn't help but wonder what I was going to tell the receptionist when she answered the phone.

That question was answered quickly when I found my phone and called the office. Before the receptionist could say anything more than hello, I blurted, "This is Ellie Sanders and I have an emergency and am headed into the office right now."

"If it's that urgent why…."

Before she could utter another word, I barked, "I need to see Dr. Lentz and only Dr. Lentz. I'll be there in fifteen minutes and I don't have time to explain." I hung up and started the car. The drive to the doctor's office was anything but calm and relaxed. Without speeding like a maniac, I maneuvered around the traffic and whipped into the parking lot where I pulled into the first empty space I spotted.

Seeing my panic-stricken face when I stormed into the office, Julia, the nurse practitioner, immediately opened the door and quickly ushered me down the hall into one of the examining rooms. My nerves were so jumpy, I couldn't sit, and, although it was only a minute or two before Dr. Lentz entered, it felt like hours, making me all the more frantic.

"So, what's the problem it couldn't wait?" he asked without wasting time.

I didn't say a word, just held up my foot.

The look of shock on his face said it all. He hesitated then said, "Get up on the table and lie down so I can look at this."

At first, I started to relax but when he didn't say anything for several minutes, I began feeling extremely anxious.

"So what is it?" I finally had the courage to ask.

"I'm not sure," he responded while turning my foot this way and that.

"Oh, great!" was all I could say.

He stood up and scratched his head. "I have an idea what it is, but I will have to research it first. If it's what I think….."

"If it's what you think, what?" I pressed.

"I don't want to say anymore until I'm sure. In the meantime, go home, relax…."

"Relax?" I shouted, "How the hell can I relax with this thing growing out of my foot? And what about the toad?"

He stared at me very seriously. "Ellie, just do as I say and I will get back to you tomorrow or the day after. If it's what I think, it is serious."

His remark sounded so ludicrous at that moment I chuckled. "Of course it's serious. How the hell can it not be?" I sat up and seeing the deep perplexed look and worry in his eyes, I knew he was sincerely concerned.

"That's it then, just go home and try to relax?"

He nodded. "Nothing will happen as long as you do that. It is not life threatening at this point…but again, I want to be certain." With that said, he left the room leaving me sitting on the examining table with pure fear coursing through my body.

I got up and left the office without stopping to say anything to anyone. I didn't want to talk. I didn't want to do anything but get whatever it was removed from my foot.

Once at home, I tried my best to take my mind off my foot. I did okay until I would feel movement and the anxiety would start all over again. It took all my will-power to not look down. When I walked from one room to another, I made it a point to keep my head up and my eyes forward. I can't even begin to describe the thoughts that raced through my mind wreaking their havoc before being replaced by a more worrisome thought.

Being transgender, I started thinking that somehow I had been given hormones that had been contaminated with amphibious DNA, and instead of developing into a woman, I was going to become some kind of mutated frog person. My imagination kicked into high gear and all I could picture was being hunted down like some grotesque hideous creature in one of Hollywood's classic B movies. Tears trickled down my cheeks. I had all I could do to shake the unnerving thoughts from my mind.

To say I was in a stupor would have been putting it mildly and I prayed with all my might that, whatever it was, Dr. Lentz would take care of it and get rid of the grotesque thing growing out of my foot. Each time the phone rang, I jumped, and each time I saw it wasn't Dr. Lentz, my hopes dwindled and I ignored the calls, letting them go to my voicemail. I was scared.

Emotionally and physically exhausted, I climbed into bed hoping beyond all hope that I would fall asleep right away and, when I awoke in the morning, I would learn it was all a dream and everything was back to normal. A part of my hope was fulfilled.

I did fall asleep right away but sometime during the night I was awakened by a weird noise. Because the sound was so out of context with the usual noises where I live, it took a moment for me to orient myself. I opened my eyes, listened and realized the noise was emanating from my foot. My first impulse was to kick the covers off and look, but to do so meant having to face the reality of what was waiting under the covers and that was entirely out of the question. Under no circumstances was I going to look at that….that thing.

To make matters worse, the deep restful sleep I so desperately needed eluded me.

The noise was just too much to bear, too much to ignore, and too loud to block out. Next morning, I was on the phone as soon as I figured the doctor's office was open. Apparently, there were instructions at the front desk to patch me right through to Dr. Lentz when I called.

"How are you doing, Ellie?" Dr. Lentz's cheerful voice echoed through the receiver.

"Not too well," I responded. "That damn thing drove me crazy all night and no matter how hard I tried, I couldn't fall asleep. Did you find any answers yet?"

I heard him take a deep breath and let out a long sigh. "No. Well not definitively anyway. But, I did find something from an old medical book I have from when I was in med school. I'm not sure whether it is the same as your situation or not, so I called an old friend and I'm waiting for a response from him. Why don't you come into the office as soon as you can? There are a couple questions I need to ask you."

Although I felt somewhat encouraged by his words, I also felt a sense of foreboding. I couldn't tell which because the tone of his voice was too matter of fact. My inability to reach a definite opinion only added to my frustration. Less than fifteen minutes later, I was sitting in the examining room waiting to hear what he had to say. I could feel my heart rate increasing and figured my blood pressure had to be through the roof, yet that seemed to pale with everything else that was taking place.

The somber look on Dr. Lentz's face when he entered the room caused my body to tense even more. He was carrying a folder and from his disheveled appearance, I guessed he had spent most of the night, if not all, doing research.

I tried to lighten the atmosphere. "You spent the night partying, huh?"

He smiled weakly then sat down and opened the folder. Just then, the phone rang and I jumped. He lifted the receiver and said, "Put him through."

"Hi, Tim. What were you able to find out? Mm-hmm, yeah, yeah, that's what I thought. Actually, she's sitting here right now. Hold on, I'll ask her."

He turned to me. "What kind of noise did you hear last night?"

I thought for a moment. "I'm not sure what kind of a noise it was. Strange is the only way I can describe it."

"Tim wants to know if you can imitate it."

I closed my eyes trying to recall the exact sounds I had heard. "Well, it was something like this – cheep, cheep, cheep uh."

I could feel my face flush with embarrassment. "Did that help?"

I waited while he listened on the phone and then I heard him say, "Okay, Tim. Thanks for the help with this. Oh yes, yes. I'll be sure to tell her. Take care."

He ended the call and turned his attention to me. "The good news is, I know your problem. The bad news is that it's what I had suspected and was just now confirmed by Tim."

"It's from the hormones, isn't it? They gave me the wrong stuff, right?"

He shook his head slowly. "No, Ellie, it's not from the hormones. Everything you've been given for your transition is exactly what you're supposed to be getting.

Besides, something like this could never be created by taking pills."

"There's a cure, right?" I asked feeling a wave of nervousness rush through my stomach.

"Yes…..I believe we can fix it."

"You mean get rid of it……right?"

"Yes, I mean get rid of it."

"Let's do it," I blurted before he had a chance to change his answer.

He held up his hand and I knew it wasn't going to be what I wanted to hear.

"It's not that simple. Let me show you what you're dealing with and then we can discuss what has to be done."

As he opened the folder, I caught a glimpse of a photo inside and quickly averted my eyes. "I don't want to see it," I heard myself softly protesting.

Dr. Lentz placed his hand on my arm in a comforting way. "Ellie, listen to me. I know this has to be difficult for you, but you have to be strong and you have to see exactly what's going on with your foot. Can you do that for me?"

I shut my eyes until I got control of my panic, then opened them and nodded.

"Good. What you have is extremely rare and ultra extremely rare to see in the United States." Pointing to the photo, he continued, "The condition is known as "Santolechae Muscaria", named after Carlos Santo, the doctor who discovered and identified it in the 1920s. Its origins are from deep within the Amazon Jungle and, to date, there have only been six reported cases. More than likely, there have been others but they were never reported, either because of lack of communication, or the victims died before they could get out of the jungle and get help."

"You're scaring me."

He looked at me very compassionately. "Forgive me, but I assure you I am not telling you this to scare you. But…. you need to understand this as best as you can. Do you need a moment or do you want me to continue?"

I glanced at the clock.

"Don't worry about the time. I've cancelled all appointments so I could go over this with you."

While I was beginning to grasp the gravity of my situation, I was also moved by him caring enough to spend the entire day devoted to my dilemma. I took a deep breath. "Go on," I said with a timid smile.

He returned my smile and flipped to a page with handwritten notes scribbled on the sides, top and bottom. "Okay, first of all, I'm going to explain what this is as best as I can. If it gets to be too much, let me know and we'll pause, but it's extremely important that you listen and understand." He studied my face until he was satisfied I was okay with what he had just said, and then continued.

"This fungus has only been found in one small remote section of the Amazon and has never been known to extend beyond that area. The only way it can be re-located is by a carrier host." He paused and stared at the wall as if trying to see something written there.

"By any chance, have you been to South America recently?"

I shook my head.

"Hmm, this is puzzling," he said and rubbed his chin. He leaned back in his chair. "This could present a whole new problem."

Not knowing what to say or think, I just stared at him. Then, as though coming out from a fog, I suddenly remembered my niece had just gotten back from South America. I sat up straight.

"My niece just returned from there. She gave me a plant that came from the jungle if that helps."

Dr. Lentz leaned forward. "Does she still have it?"

I frowned. "No. As a matter of fact, I was the one who accidentally knocked it over and broke the plant and the pot. I felt terrible about it."

He placed his hand on my wrist. "Did you come in contact with the soil?"

"Yeah, it was all over my foot."

"The foot with the growth?" he pressed.

"Yes, how did you know?"

He took a deep breath. " According to the reports and limited studies that have been done, when the adult female toad gets pregnant, she burrows into a mature toadstool, which has the ability to host the toad without dying. The toad then follows the roots and deposits its eggs. Once that's accomplished, she returns to the main plant and dies thus feeding the toadstool. The eggs remain protected within the root. The offshoot itself grows until it finds a host plant to attach to both for an anchor and to absorb nutrients. Sometimes the eggs transfer to the new host where they remain dormant for an unspecified period of time. When the eggs do hatch, they make their way to the top and begin searching for a mate. They do this by making the noises you described. The cycle then repeats itself."

"I know you'd like something stronger right about now, but all I can offer is water. Would you like some?" he asked and stood up.

"Yes, please," I answered and realized my mouth had dried up like a wad of cotton.

A couple minutes later, he returned with two bottles of water and handed one to me. I practically had to force myself to drink it slowly and not give in to my urge to gulp it down. I glanced at Dr. Lentz and observed as he twisted the page this way and that as he read the notes. Noticing I was watching him, he set the paper down.

"Are you ready to continue?"

I nodded. "So how did I get it?"

He leaned back in the chair again and folded his hands in his lap. "When you broke the pot and the plant itself, you must have released the hatched egg and it immediately bored its way into you."

"I didn't feel a thing though."

"That could be because you were concentrating on cleaning up the mess and probably apologizing profusely that you didn't notice. Also, we're not sure about this but there's a consensus that the toad has the ability to produce a numbing agent in its saliva so the live host doesn't feel it entering."

I didn't like what I was hearing but I understood it. "That explains the toad; How about the mushroom?"

"There's only one small article about that but it makes sense and is the only explanation we have. According to that study, when the egg is in the root of the toadstool, it feeds on the fibers and absorbs enough of the plant DNA to be able to grow another host plant. Apparently, the toad is able to store this DNA until it is absolutely necessary to release it through its urine or feces, we're not sure which, thereby securing its own survival."

He paused to take a drink of water. "That, unfortunately, is the easy part of this problem."

"What do you mean?" I interrupted, wanting and not wanting to hear what he was going to say next.

"The problem lies in extracting it from your foot and—"

"Oh God, don't tell me you can't get rid of this thing. Please tell me you can cure me. Please," I begged him.

Once again he softly touched my hand. "You can be cured but it's not going to be easy."

"How difficult can it be? Just cut it out," I said, trying to control the panic coursing through my body.

Dr. Lentz dropped his head for a moment and I realized that whatever it was he was trying to tell me, it was just as difficult for him to say it as it was going to be for me to hear it.

"I'm sorry," I apologized. "I don't mean to put more pressure on you."

He glanced at me, patted my hand and nodded. "The only way you can remove this is by going to South America and finding the area where these things exist. This is their mating season and it needs to find a mate. Once it does, it will leave your foot. At that point, the toadstool will begin to die and then we can remove it. During the mating season, however, the toads are very dangerous and very aggressive. They also contain some type of poison that they can administer through their saliva and that's why we can't even attempt to remove it now."

Somehow, whether from being in shock; stunned by what he said; pure amazement and disbelief; or numb from being so panic-stricken, I remained calm. I took a sip of water and just stared at the wall above his head.

"What if it doesn't find a mate?" I heard myself asking from some distant place and wasn't sure if I had actually said it out loud or if it was just in my mind.

He rubbed his face with both hands and replied, "We just don't know. There haven't been enough cases to formulate any concrete evidence or to even postulate what could happen and, without something to go on, we can't risk your life."

"Can't you just kill it or knock it out or something?"

"We might be able to if we could get at it. The problem with that is, if we fail to catch it right away, it could poison you knowing it's being attacked. I'm afraid to say it, but both Tim and I agree that the only way to do this is the way I explained it to you."

He took a long pull on the water bottle, nearly emptying it before he spoke again. "I want you to think hard before answering. Have you told anyone about this?"

I thought that was a strange question, but I sifted through my memory and responded, "No, I haven't told anyone but you."

"You're positive?"

"Yes, I'm positive. Why?"

He cleared his throat. "Ellie, what I'm about to tell you next is extremely important that you follow it to the letter. You cannot and, I repeat, cannot tell anyone about this, including your niece."

I started to say something, but he shut me down with a wave of his hand.

"Here are the reasons why. Firstly, if word of this gets out and the right people hear about it, you could find yourself being an unwilling guinea pig for experimental purposes and your life would be the least considered element. Secondly, you would not be able to leave the country. And lastly, if left untreated, you will probably die like the others."

He took both my hands in his. "The good news, if it can be labeled as such, is that Tim Hastings, my colleague to whom I was speaking on the phone, will be going with you to South America. Tim knows more about this than anyone else. You will be escorting him as his student under the presumption you are there to study some of the fungi and amphibians of the region. If you agree to this, your plane leaves at 2a.m. tomorrow. Tim will pick you up and, on the way to the airport, he will brief you on what to expect and what to say to whomever."

"Now, do you agree?"

Tears trickled down my cheeks and all I could do was nod.

Dr. Lentz stood up, helped me from my seat and hugged me. "You're a courageous woman, Ellie. Remember that. Tim's a very gentle, compassionate person and very capable of taking care of you, so trust him."

He stepped back and stared down at me. "Are you going to be okay?"

"Yes," I whispered.

"Any questions you want to ask before you go?"

I forced a little smile to my lips.

Dr. Lentz smiled and said, "Probably a million of them I suspect."

When I didn't say anything, he added, "Well, if you think of any, don't hesitate to call. I'll be here for the rest of the day. Oh, let me give you my cell number in case you can't reach me here."

He leaned over the desk, tore a page off a prescription pad, wrote his number and handed it to me. "When you get home, try to relax. Hold on." He took the paper from my hand. "I forgot to give you Tim's number." A moment later, he handed the paper back and escorted me to the outside door. "Don't forget; call if you need me, even if it's just to talk."

Impulsively, I rose up on my toes, kissed him on the cheek, then turned and left the office. The drive home was a big blur and I was thankful for not having any other added extra stress on my mind.

In the house, I moved around like a robot mechanically gathering things for the trip. I located a pair of hiking boots which were ideal for hiding my foot and for the pretense of being a student on a field trip through the jungle. When I placed the last article of clothing in the suitcase, I zipped it up and plopped down on the couch. I was exhausted.

I barely heard the phone ringing and realized I had fallen asleep. I glanced at the clock. It showed 12:45 a.m. The number on the caller ID was unfamiliar and I was about to ignore it when I remembered that Tim was supposed to call.

"Hello," I said in a muzzy voice while still trying to clear the cobwebs from my mind.

"Hello. Is this Ellie?" the voice asked.

"Yes it is. Is this Tim?"

"Yes, I'm sorry to wake you but I wanted to let you know I'm on my way to your house now. We have to get to the airport early enough to go through the scanning and whatever other nonsensical thing they do."

"I'm all packed and ready," I replied.

"Good, I'll see you in a few," he finished and hung up.

The airport wasn't crowded when we arrived and everything went smoothly and quickly, including the boarding. Neither Tim nor I said much in the car on the way to the airport, and I was appreciative of his letting me absorb things without distraction.

The flight to South America was uneventful and Tim spent almost the entire flight explaining what I needed to know if asked any questions by customs officers or other officials. He stressed how imperative it was for me to be prepared so no questions would be asked about our intentions. He reiterated more than once that the last thing we wanted to do was to draw suspicion by my uncertainty. We went over everything again and again until he felt satisfied that I would handle things okay. He also assured me that he would do most all of the talking and would try his best to deflect the attention away from me.

Waiting in line at customs, I could feel the butterflies frolicking in my stomach as though they were on holiday and no matter how hard I tried to quell them, they persisted entertaining center stage. As it turned out, my concerns and worries were unnecessary because the officer who checked my luggage looked as though he didn't want to be there and passed me right on through.

Outside the terminal, we were greeted by two young men and a young woman. Tim introduced them as, Mike, Fernando and Carlotta, three graduate students working in a lab not far from the area we needed to get to. Fernando pointed to what looked like an extended Jeep and he and Tim climbed into the front while the rest of us took the seats in back.

The ride from the airport was relatively smooth until about 45 minutes into the trip when Fernando turned onto a dirt road. It didn't take long before I was being jostled around and had to hang on tightly to one of the roll bars so I wouldn't be thrown from the vehicle. I glanced at the others and saw them doing the same thing. Mentally, I didn't feel so bad, but I was certain my buttocks and thighs were going to be black and blue before we reached the lab.

We drove for another two hours through and around large puddles and potholes. Finally, Carlotta pointed to an area beyond the front of the Jeep. In the distance, I could see a clearing with what appeared to be a small building. I looked back at Carlotta and we exchanged smiles, both happy and relieved the torture was over. A couple minutes later we reached our destination. The lab was much larger than how it had appeared from a distance.

"You do this every day?" I asked Carlotta as we climbed from the Jeep.

She laughed. "God no, I wouldn't be able to tolerate it. We pretty much limit our traveling to when we need supplies. During the rainy season, we hardly go anywhere because the road floods and some spots are just too deep to try to get through."

Mike retrieved my suitcase and was carrying it in for me. I stopped to look at the scenery. When he saw me standing there, he called out, "Don't stay too long or the bugs will get you and you don't want to risk getting a disease out here."

I trotted to catch up to him. "Thanks," I said.

The inside of the building was surprisingly pleasant, clean and orderly. Carlotta motioned for me to follow her and we walked down a hallway and entered the living quarters. The atmosphere was warm and friendly and had a woman's touch to it. If it hadn't been for the ride through the jungle, it could easily have passed as someone's home in the States.

Fernando cooked that night and Carlotta explained how they all took turns with the chores. I truly enjoyed speaking about our plans for the next day's trek and especially that no one asked me about my foot. They asked a lot of questions about back home and each gave a brief synopsis of how they came to be here at the lab. They were a fascinating group and I was glad my mind was occupied with other things besides my foot.

The reprieve was short-lived, however, because no sooner had I gotten into bed, the toad began its mating call once again. I'm not sure how long it kept up its song because I was too exhausted to be disturbed by it. I fell into a deep sleep and didn't hear a thing. Morning came too quickly. If it hadn't been for Carlotta persistently shaking me, I would have kept right on sleeping. My backside was stiff and sore from the previous day's journey. Luckily, I had brought some ibuprofen with me and hoped it would work quickly.

The atmosphere in the main room was quiet compared to the night before. As soon as we finished eating, Carlotta checked my clothing to make sure I was properly prepared for our trek into the jungle. That done, we headed out for what I desperately hoped would be the end of my nightmare.

Making our way through the jungle was slow and arduous. Several times we were

brought to a complete halt until the men cleared a path. The thick growth forced us to walk in single file. Mike took the lead, followed by Carlotta, Tim, and myself. Fernando brought up the rear. I could feel the heat and humidity sapping my strength and before long, my clothes were soaked with sweat. Periodically Mike stopped long enough for us to take drinks of water and to catch our breath.

Two and a half hours later, Mike turned to the rest of us. "We're here, but we can't go any further. Remember to remain quiet or we'll spook them which would mean we'd have to come back tomorrow and, I for one don't want to do that."

Mike motioned for me to step forward. "The rest is up to you," he whispered. "You have to remove your boot and then slowly stick your foot under these bushes." He pointed to the closest bush and said, "That space underneath should be large enough for you to slowly push your foot through."

I knelt down and started unlacing my boot and glanced at the space where I had to shove my foot. When I realized I wouldn't be able to see my foot or have any idea what was going to happen to it once it was through, I shivered. A wave of panic washed over me. Knowing I would have no idea what was happening was the worst part of all. For all I knew, there could have been a jungle troll on the other side that loved eating toadstools and would see my foot as a feast.

Sensing my fear, Carlotta knelt down beside me. "You have to do it, Ellie. I know it's not easy but it's the only way you can get rid of this thing. I'll sit with you if you want."

I nodded. "Thanks."

The moment had arrived. I sat on the rubber sheet Mike had placed beneath me and carefully eased my foot through the opening. When I felt no resistance, I stopped and hoped I had gotten it far enough through to do the trick. Carlotta placed her arm around my shoulders and leaned her head against mine.

While we waited, my thoughts drifted to all the emotional, mental, physical, medical and societal struggles I had gone through while transitioning. I came to the conclusion that none of those anxieties invoked the fear and worry that this ordeal was putting me through.

After what seemed like forever, I felt a stirring in my foot and wondered if the troll had come to dinner. We heard the toad's mating call and my stomach muscles tightened. I had all I could do to whisper to everyone what was happening. Fernando began writing in his pad, wanting to record the events for future reference.

Carlotta turned her head so her mouth was near my ear. "Can you feel anything different?" she asked. "I mean, are you in pain?"

Afraid of talking too much, I just shook my head.

I'm not sure how much time had gone by before I started to feel a stirring around and on my foot. We also heard the excited rhythmic song of the toad. I had the greatest temptation to scream, believing the troll had arrived. It took all of my will power to fight off the urge to yank my foot back. I grabbed Carlotta's hand and squeezed it tightly. Almost as quickly as it had started, everything stopped, including the noise.

None of us could see through the bushes and had no idea what was happening.

I glanced at Tim. "Should I pull my foot out now?" I whispered.

He held his hand up and flashed his fingers signaling five more minutes. I wanted to kill him, but I remembered Dr. Lentz's words to trust him. I resigned myself to waiting it out. In the meantime, I shifted my head back and forth from my ankle to Tim and back again.

Tim finally motioned for me to withdraw my foot. Carlotta squeezed my hand and we all held our breath hoping nothing would go wrong. Fighting the urge to yank my foot back, I carefully eased it out of the bush.

Tim stepped forward and gently lifted my foot. He moved it from side to side, then examined the sole for any odd bumps or lumps. He kept his fingers on the sole of my foot for a few minutes and nodded.

"I don't feel anything. I think it's safe to say we were successful," Tim said reassuringly.

"When will you be sure?" I blurted thickly, my mouth dry from nerves.

"My guess is tonight," Tim said. "If it's still inside your foot, it will start its song all over again. If nothing happens, I would say it's safe to posit it's gone."

I looked him in the eyes and smiled. "Spoken like a true scientist."

When I said that, the others breathed a sigh of relief and Fernando was the first to speak. "Ready to head back then? This place gives me the creeps."

"It gives all of us the creeps," Carlotta added and the other two men agreed.

Tim held his hand out to help me up. "You ready?"

Wanting to get out of there, I probably could have rocketed to my feet, but I was appreciative of the offer and took his hand.

That night, there was no disquieting toad song and I was able to drift into a peaceful slumber. Early the next morning, after a few phone calls, we were back in the Jeep heading for the airport. We arrived in plenty of time to check in and get all our paperwork stamped. I cried, hugged everyone and beat them all with my "thanks" for having saved my life.

The flight back home was more relaxing than when we had departed for the Amazon. When we exited the plane, Dr. Lentz was waiting for us. He told Tim that he would be escorting me to the clinic to get the toadstool x-rayed, and, if all was well, removed. Needless to say, I was relieved and excited at the speed with which he wanted to remove the growth. Then, entering the clinic, I immediately spotted the medical staff waiting to take care of me and I cried tears of joy.

The Envelope

Just as Terri stepped from the office building to the sidewalk, she spotted her bus pulling away from the curb. It blended in with the moving traffic and she knew she had no chance of catching up to it. If she hadn't stopped to use the ladies room, she would have been on time. She checked her watch and realized she wasn't at fault. The bus had come early. Now she would have to wait half an hour for the next bus or walk three blocks to catch a bus from there, which would drop her off a little over a block away from where her usual bus stopped.

She started walking and felt a shiver from the cold wind that seemed to have picked up. Turning her collar up and buttoning the top button on her coat, Terri wished summer was only days away instead of months.

In the middle of the second block, she spotted a man stooped down with his arms wrapped across his chest to keep warm. He looked up at her and didn't say a word, just nodded. The sadness in his eyes said it all and she shivered again but not from the cold. At the corner coffee shop she bought a large coffee and a bagel. Before stepping back outside, she removed an envelope from her briefcase and placed a twenty dollar bill inside and sealed it. Terri backtracked to where the man was still squatting.

She paused in front of him and when he looked up, she said, "I thought you might enjoy this since it is getting so much colder. It may help to keep you warm."

She then handed him the coffee, the bag with the bagel and the envelope.

"Thank you," he smiled weakly and took the items from her outstretched hands.

"You're welcome," she replied and turned and walked away. On the next block, two nuns sat behind a small table with a sign on it that read, "Please help the poor."

Terri started to walk past then stopped, reached into her pocket and pulled out the two 1 dollar bills she had gotten in change at the coffee shop. She stuffed them into the slot in the locked box on the table.

The nuns smiled, thanked her and in unison said, "May God bless you."

Terri turned and proceeded to the corner and joined a small group of people waiting for the bus. The nuns' words repeated themselves in her mind and she thought about how she had stopped believing in God, when her son, Michael told her and his father that he was really a girl. He said he was transgender and was going to change his name to Michelle.

As much as Terri didn't understand how that could be, she accepted and embraced him. Michael's father, however, was the complete opposite. He started beating Michael, often for no other reason than venting his anger and disgust for him. His cruelty toward Michael was not just physical, but mental as well. When he wasn't hitting Michael, he tormented him mercilessly by insulting and berating him. He called Michael every derogatory name he could think of and constantly told Michael he was useless and no good.

Before his father died, Michael moved out of the house when he was old enough and never contacted either of them again.

At first, Terri prayed incessantly, asking God to return Michelle, but to no avail. After the 4th year, with her hopes diminished, she prayed less and less until she finally prayed no more. Hope, as far as she was concerned, was somewhere far beyond the horizon. She had lost the son she'd given birth to and the daughter she never got to know.

Turning to look back toward the nuns, Terri noticed the man she had helped holding the coffee and bagel out to someone in one of the doorways. A moment later, a small gray haired woman, Terri hadn't noticed, stepped from the doorway and took the coffee and bag. She then reached out and touched his arm and he tenderly bent down and kissed her head. The man then moved toward the table with the box for donations for the poor and Terri watched him stuff the envelope she had given him in the slot, before turning and disappearing into the crowd.

Unable to resist her curiosity, Terri hurried back to the table and asked the nuns, "Do you know that man?"

Both nuns smiled and the shorter of the two answered, "Yes, he's an angel."

"Thank you," was all Terri said. She returned to the corner in time to catch the bus. On the trip home, she couldn't help thinking about the cliché the nun had used to describe the man who had put the envelope in the box. Terri smiled. She imagined that, to the nuns, everyone who made a donation was an angel.

It wasn't until later that night when Terri was cuddled on the couch with her afghan, drinking a hot cup of coffee that the day's events struck her. The nuns had been right. That man was an angel. Terri had bought him a coffee and a bagel from the loose bills she had jammed into her pocket that morning. As for the twenty dollars, she could well afford it, so the reality of the sacrifice she thought she had made turned out to not be a sacrifice at all.

That man, however, made the true sacrifice. He gave the coffee and bagel to a woman he felt needed it more than he. The twenty dollars, which would have been enough to get a cheap bed for the night, he instead gave to those he believed were needier.

Terri sunk a little lower in the couch and shook her head. From the time she had gotten on the bus to just a few minutes before, she had praised herself for the kindness she had shown. She had patted herself on the back thinking what a good deed she had done. But now, she knew her actions paled in comparison to the selfless generosity the man showed toward others. He gave without so much as wanting praise or a pat on the back. He gave from his heart not his wallet. He gave his all and gave it willingly.

Terri turned her head, looked toward the fireplace and spotted the small crucifix hanging above the mantel. She shivered. Maybe, just maybe, she had been in the presence of a real angel. She shrugged her shoulders, finished her coffee and went to bed.

The next morning, while on her way to work, Terri watched for the man, but she never spotted him. The nuns at the table were different from the nuns who were there the day before. Terri's day passed without incident and again, on the way home, she looked to see if she could spot the man with the sad eyes, but as in the morning, he was nowhere in sight.

That night, sitting in her favorite spot on the couch, while sipping a glass of wine, the phone rang. She looked at the number. She didn't recognize it at all and figured it would be a telemarketer.

"Hello," she said with an attitude.

The person on the other end cleared their throat before saying, "Mom?"

Terri sat up straight. "Michael...uh...Michelle? Is it really you?"

"Can I come home?"

Terri choked back the tears in her eyes and the lump forming in her throat. "Mmmi...Michelle, yes, yes, yes. You can come home! Where are you?"

"I'll be there in five minutes," Michelle answered and hung up.

Terri sprang from the couch and starting pacing. "Oh my God. Oh my God," was all she was capable of saying at the moment.

Even though she knew Michelle would be there any moment, Terri jumped when the doorbell rang. Terri took deep breaths trying to exhale slowly in an effort to maintain her composure. She hurried to the door and pulled it open. Michelle stood for a moment before entering the house.

As soon as the door was closed, Terri threw her arms around her daughter and cried uncontrollably. Moments later, Michelle cried with her. The two remained like that for a few minutes before Terri pulled back and studied her. Michelle was older but she looked great.

"You look beautiful," Terri said in spite of the number of questions racing through her mind. She forced herself not to pepper Michelle with them and not to put pressure on her to explain. She was home and that was all that mattered.

Terri made coffee for both of them. She also made some toast with butter and grape jelly, a favorite of Michelle's when she was living at home. She sat across from Michelle and waited patiently for her to share what she wanted to talk about.

After her second slice of toast, Michelle looked at her mother and said, "The strangest thing happened a couple days ago. I was thinking of you and home and feeling like I wanted to be here. I got on a bus and was on my way here when sometime during the trip I fell asleep and someone stole what little money I had from my duffel bag. I didn't know it until I got to the next bus terminal and couldn't buy a ticket.

"I figured I would just have to hitchhike the rest of the way. I didn't even have enough money to buy a coffee and had to ask a couple people for some change. It was rather embarrassing. While I was there, this guy came up to me, handed me an envelope and walked away. At first, I thought he was one of those Jesus freaks you always hear about lurking around the bus or train stations, but when I opened the envelope, there was a twenty dollar bill in it."

Terri buried her face in her hands and burst out crying. Michelle didn't have to describe the man or say anymore because she knew in her heart he was the man she had given the envelope to. The one the nuns called an angel.

Michelle moved to her and put her arms around her shoulders. "Mom, are you okay? Did I say something wrong?"

With tear-stained cheeks Terri glanced up at her and said, "No, Honey, you didn't say anything wrong at all. You said the perfect thing. Thanks to an angel, I have my faith in God and you in my home and heart again.

An Unexpected Lesson

Wanting change in my life, I decided to travel down South for the holiday season. Now, being a New Englander, and, in spite of my not being a worldly traveler, I know I don't live in a vacuum. In fact, I like to think of myself as being fairly knowledgeable about the many facets of lifestyles. I honestly didn't believe that there was any one particular circumstance that could surprise or shock me. How wrong I was!

Feeling adventurous, I chose to explore the back hills of West Virginia and Tennessee. Needless to say, I ventured onto one of those old, winding, country mountain roads and got myself so twisted up I didn't know if I was coming or going. After an hour of aimlessly wandering around, I had to accept defeat and admit to myself I was lost.

I didn't get discouraged because, after all, I was exploring and it was supposed to be an adventure. At least I kept trying to convince myself of that. It was at this point I spotted a dirt road that had all the signs of having been traveled quite a bit, so I took a deep breath and turned onto it. As the road meandered up through the woods, I began to question my sanity thinking that at any moment I would be mistaken for an IRS agent and shot by moonshiners.

I have to tell you that this line of thinking can be detrimental to one's mental stability, especially for a person who has an active imagination to begin with. Before I could stop myself from letting my thoughts get frantically out of control, I had conjured up a whole scenario that would have made the movie "Deliverance" seem like a "boys will be boys" Boy Scout movie. As you can imagine, within moments, I had worked myself into a state of paranoia. I was convinced I was going to die. Little did I know that that wrong turn would be the right turn in changing my outlook forever.

Just as I was about to stop and shift the car into reverse and try to back down the road, I entered a clearing where an old shack came into view. I breathed a sigh of relief knowing I could make a U-turn and get the heck out of there. Not to be.

Halfway into the turn, someone came out of the shack carrying a rifle and waved for me to stop. At the sight of the gun, my mind went into chaos and all hell broke out inside my body. My heart beat inside my chest so hard I thought it was going to explode. My skin immediately felt cold and clammy. My right hand shook so violently it knocked the gearshift into neutral, stopping the car. At the same time, my foot pressed hard on the gas pedal causing the engine to roar like one of the NASCAR racers at the Indy 500. I screamed loud enough to scare the crap out of a banshee.

The person holding the rifle stepped to the front of my car and stopped. Once I calmed down, I was able to see clearly and I know, without a doubt, my jaw dropped open. In front of me stood a hairy, six-foot man wearing a polka dot dress and clod-hopper boots, sporting a scruffy beard and what appeared to be long yellow hair fashioned from a scraggly-looking mop head.

He motioned with the rifle barrel for me to get out of the car. I did as he gestured. I thought for sure I was going to get shot right then and there. Instead, he stepped around to the side of the car and stuck out his big, beefy, calloused hand to shake mine.

I nervously placed my small hand in his and watched as it got swallowed up by his thick fingers. I waited for the mighty squeeze and the crunch of breaking bones but that didn't come. I must admit that I was amazed by the tender, gentle way he shook my hand. "Name's Glen, but you can call me Glenda." When I looked up, I was greeted by a big speckled-toothed grin.

I couldn't help smiling nervously and I believe the big fellow took it as a friendly gesture because he lowered the gun. In a deep-husky voice said, "C'mon inside. Coffee's on the stove."

He took two steps, stopped and glanced up toward the roof and bellowed, "Granny, c'mon down we got ourselves a visitor."

He must have noticed the shocked expression on my face and simply said, "She's been up there all mornin' cleanin' that dang chimney. If tweren't for feedin' ol' Jeb, she'd be up there all dang day. Well, never you mind, she'll be down right quick. She loves havin' visitors."

The inside of the house was dark and the only light, besides the little bit coming in through the windows, was from a kerosene lamp on the small wooden table. Before I could take another step into the house, a large, fat pig came running out of the darkness and headed right for me. I let out a yelp and jumped to the side just in time to avoid being knocked out the door.

Glenda whacked it on the nose with the butt of the rifle. "Get in your corner, ya crazy damn ol' pig."

He turned to me. "You okay?"

While keeping my eyes on the pig, I nodded.

"This here's Jebediah, but we call 'im Jeb lessin' he gets too crazy, then we call him a lot of other names. Granny does most o' that, bein' as I'm tryin' ta be a lady an' all."

Just then, Granny stepped into the house. "I see ya met ol' Jeb, and....." she paused and with a sarcastic tone, continued, "Gl-e-n-d-a. He thinks he's a transmutant. Got the crazy notion from watchin' some guy named Ponvict on the T.V. box in town."

Glenda plunked the coffee mugs down hard on the table. "It's not transmutant. It's transgender. I keep tellin' ya that. And it's not Ponvict. It's Povich ---- Maury Povich."

"Don't make a dang bit o' difference what his name is, he's got ya dancin' and prancin' round like a Mary Jane."

Glenda huffed. "I ain't prancin' and I ain't a Mary Jane. Sides, we got us a visitor and twouldn't be polite ta argue in front of 'er."

Granny wrinkled her face at him and shook her head from side to side, then turned to me. "Would ya like a biscuit with ya coffee, Miss?"

I realized at that point I hadn't introduced myself. Not sure what they'd do if I didn't, I blurted, "Teresa Miller, but you can just call me Terry."

I took the biscuit and surprisingly, both it and the coffee were real tasty. Granny practically gulped down her coffee and said, "I best be getting' back to that chimney." She went out and a couple minutes later, I heard her on the roof.

As I sat drinking my coffee, I couldn't help but feel sad for Glenda and how she must have felt. I realized that my perception of where and how transgender people lived was completely incorrect. Living in the city, it was somewhat common for me to hear about transgender people and how they are often times forced into the sex trade or how they have been so rejected by family, friends and society as a whole that they commit suicide. I never heard anyone talk about what it was like for a transgender person who lived in the rural towns of America or, in this case, the backwoods.

"Is somethin' wrong?" I heard Glenda asking.

"No," I answered then said, "Yes. Yes, actually there is."

"It's because of me, isn't it?" Glenda said, her shoulders slumping and her chin lowered to her chest.

"Yes, but not in the way you think," I reassured her.

Glenda raised her head and looked at me questioningly.

I took another mouthful of coffee. "It must be very difficult for you," I said hoping I wasn't going to offend her.

Glenda smiled her speckled-tooth grin. "Oh ya mean cuz of granny?"

I nodded.

Glenda sat up straight and with a sparkle in her eyes said, "Granny says lots of things 'bout it, but she means no harm." Looking down, Glenda smoothed her hands over her stomach. "She's the one got me my dress."

Glenda must have seen the look of shock on my face. "Granny luvs me. My ma an' pa died from pneumonia when I was just a youngin' and granny's been takin' care o' me since."

Fascinated, I asked, "What about the people in town? What do they think?"

Glenda got up, picked up the coffee pot and filled both our cups. When she sat down, she flashed another smile at me. "The folks in town don't pay me much mind anymore."

"But they did at one time?" I asked.

Glenda nodded. "Yep, they sure 'nough did. That was when I was a good size smaller. I'm bigger an' stronger than most now so they leave me alone. I know they talk 'bout me an' laugh behind my back an' all, but I don't pay 'em no mind."

"Does it bother you to be so big?" I asked, wanting to know about her.

She didn't respond at first and I thought I had overstepped my bounds, but then she looked over at me with a gleam in her eyes and said, "I know I don' have a good education an' all, but I'm smart 'nough to know I won' ever look like you or granny an' that's okay cuz I know….." she paused and then, as erect and square-shouldered as could be, continued, "I know deep down inside, I'm just as much a woman as any other woman."

The sincerity and conviction of her words touched my heart so much that it brought tears to my eyes. I got up, walked over, hugged her and said, "I'm so proud of you."

We talked a while longer and then I said I had to get going. Glenda gave me directions on which way to go so I could get back to the main road. I bid my farewell and headed out.

A half hour later, I turned right onto a road that was only paved for the first 100 yards and then became a dirt road. A feeling of déjà vu swept over me and I immediately panicked. I was in no condition to deal with another attacking pig or whatever else lurked up ahead, so I jammed on the brakes.

I shifted into reverse and gunned the car back down the road with surprising accuracy. Not long after, I spotted a sign that directed me to the highway, but instead of continuing south, I followed the route north. I remember thinking at the time that maybe a holiday in New England wasn't such a bad thing after all.

For many months following that vacation, I kept thinking about Glenda and I would smile and sometimes laugh aloud, but I would also find myself thinking about how sadly disconnected it must have been for her. I'm sure her life could not have been easy. I had made it a point to get Glenda's address while I was there and mailed her a package with a dress and a beautiful wig I thought would compliment her features.

Since that time, I have come to learn that transgender people come from all walks of life and many, if not all transgender people, live a complicated life. Not only do they face the scorn and ridicule of society, but they risk the loss of love and support from family and friends. Equally stressful is the psychological struggles they must also endure with having to live a duality of emotions.

As I have become more educated on transgender issues and met other transgender people, I have come to understand that in spite of all they must cope with, there is also a tremendous joy and happiness when they are finally free to live their lives as they were meant to be. Those thoughts always bring me back to Glenda and how thrilled and happy she was being herself in a backwoods part of the country tucked away with a feisty grandmother and a crazy old fat pig named Jebediah.

Are You For Real?

Have you ever had something happen to you that you just couldn't explain no matter how hard you try? Something so bizarre you know people would label you as insane if you were to tell them? I have had two such experiences in my lifetime. The first was when I knew at 5 years old that I was a girl instead of the boy my mother gave birth to. Yes, I am transgender. I don't know how I knew, I just did. I never was able to explain it then, and, to be quite honest, I still can't explain it fully now. The fact is, I am transgender and have had all the surgeries required to help me live my life as it should be, and over the course of time, people have accepted me for who I am.

The second thing I experienced is not quite as acceptable to overcome. This one I can't even begin to explain no matter how hard I have tried. With that in mind, I thought I'd take the risk of sharing with you what happened to me; and show you how my imagination took a leap beyond the believable.

It was a beautiful spring day and I was thinking, finally, some warmer weather! Days before, I was convinced after the winter seemed to drag on longer than usual that spring was never going to come to my little New England town. For me, I was eager to get out in it, maybe do some shopping, even if only window-shopping. I loved looking for the newest fashions and especially enjoyed finding the clearance items, whether last year's styles or not.

Deciding to get an early start on my day, I headed off downtown to browse the stores for sales, hoping to find something marked down that would fit my budget. Main Street is a quaint little strip with a variety of small shops. Everything from clothing boutiques, barbershop, beauty salon, drug store and a hardware store are right there. There's even a movie theater. Everyone is friendly in that small town way, and while we have to travel to the larger retail giants sometimes, most of the town folk get there wares right here.

I decided to step into Marlee's Fashions for a quick glance to see if anything new had arrived since my last visit. I am somewhat hesitant at times because my grandmother told me stories about things she said happened in her life, and I grew up wondering whether they were just stories or if she had really experienced them. In the end, I loved her, so it didn't really matter. Besides, it was her storytelling ability that planted itself into my mind, and I have no doubt that is where and how my imagination developed.

Marlee's is a consignment shop. She had opened the store when she was in her 40s that slowly, thanks to a good economy, grew into a full retail store. I like shopping there because it's not overcrowded, making it very easy to peruse the merchandise on the racks. In spite of the store not being large, there is a nice selection of clothes, and Marlee tries her best to make sure the styles are close to the newest trends.

Toward the rear of the shop, on a circular rack, I spotted a rust-colored blouse with a delicate lace trim and hurried to check it out. When I looked at the tag, I discovered it was not my size. The blouse was exactly what I was looking for to match a skirt I had picked up a couple of weeks before. Not one to give up, I searched the nearby racks hoping to see another one. My heart raced when I thought I spotted one on the rack near the back wall tucked in the corner.

Reaching the area, I pushed the clothes aside to get to the blouse I'd seen and noticed something written on the wall behind it. It looked to be graffiti at first, but when I was able to get a clearer view of it, I realized it was a poem of sorts. Intrigued, I read it and then retrieved a pen and pad from my purse to copy it down. This is what I copied:

About time you got here. I've
Been waiting for you,
Carmen.
Do you know what
Events await
For you to see?
Got your interest
Haven't
I?
Just so you'll know
Keep reading
Lest you want to die.
My my you are
Not going to ignore this note
Or
Possibly dismiss it as a lunatic's
Quote?
Remember I am the one who
Stated your name.
Think before you
Underestimate my

Veracity and burden the blame.
While being labeled a
Xerxes or worse.
Yielding your mind becoming
Zany and forever cursed.

My first reaction, of course, was to look around to see if someone was playing a joke, but then I couldn't explain how that was possible since no one, including myself, knew I was going to be in the store that day. I knew I hadn't been online that morning, so there was no one in my social circle that I would have shared that I was going shopping.

I pushed the clothes together blocking out the message and then, for whatever reason, I opened the space again -- only to find a blank wall. I glanced down at the words I had written on my pad. I had to get out of there and made a beeline for the front of the store, completely forgetting about the blouse.

I went across the street into Tracy's Coffee & Sandwich Shop and was grateful I didn't have to wait in line. I ordered a coffee and went outside where I found a bench underneath some Japanese maple trees to sit down and ponder what had just happened.

Putting on my sunglasses, I glanced around as inconspicuously as possible to see if anyone was nearby recording my actions, but no one appeared to be doing anything out of the ordinary. I resumed studying the writing trying to make some kind of determination about it and would have thrown it out except for the fact it had my name in it. There was no way it could have been there by coincidence. Forty-five minutes later and frustrated from going round and round in a circle with it, I stuffed the message inside my pocketbook and headed for home.

It was close to an hour later before I sat down at the kitchen table with the piece of paper again, hoping to find something meaningful that would make sense. Such was not the case. Having absolutely no success, I put it down and tried to ignore it. I emphasize "tried" because it was like being a person who's on a diet, staring at a piece of chocolate cake on a plate in front of them, knowing that eating the cake would only serve to ruin the diet, while at the same time, dwelling on all the delicious reasons to take a bite.

Giving in to my curiosity, I let my eyes drift down to the poem again and realized that the first letter of each line was written in alphabetical order. I verified my discovery by counting the lines to be sure and there were twenty-six. Needless to say, this piqued my interest even more and breathed new life into my wanting to decipher its meaning. Three hours, two cups of coffee and a cup of tea later, I was no further ahead in deciphering its meaning than when I had first begun. To say it was aggravating would be a stupendous understatement. When I'd had enough self-punishment, I left the house to run some errands. The break was incredibly relaxing and I tried my best not to think about the poem on my kitchen table.

When I returned home, I decided to make one last-ditch effort to root out the meaning within the lines, but before I could sink my teeth into the task, I was interrupted by an unexpected knock on the door. As far as I knew, I hadn't ordered anything, nor had anyone called to say they were stopping by.

I opened the door and came face to face with a complete stranger. He was average looking with short black hair, clean shaven, wearing a white casual shirt and gray slacks. Normally, I would have thought nothing of it, but before I could say anything, he said, "I am from the future and if need be, I can prove it."

I had all I could do to keep from laughing in his face. Instinctively, I moved to the side with the intention of closing the door, but something, I'm not quite sure what, made me pause. In doing so, I couldn't help noticing how the sunlight reflecting on his features was similar to the way it used to shine on my grandfather's face. In fact, the man resembled one of my uncles so I figured he was one of my relatives I hadn't yet met and the family, probably knowing about my fascination with my grandmother's tales, was playing a joke on me. What else could it have been? After all, it was the only logical explanation I could come up with at the time.

I scanned the street for signs of one or more of them sitting in a nearby car or standing in a doorway having a good laugh at my expense. Seeing no one, I turned my attention back to the fellow patiently waiting on my doorstep.

I invited him in. "So, what's this all about?" I asked, trying my best to keep from laughing.

He glanced around my small apartment and then motioned to one of the chairs at the table. I nodded and he casually moved to the chair and sat down. Once seated, he said, "You have to go to the Ho Ling's Chinese Laundry in Boston's Chinatown, or you will die".

Unable to contain myself any longer, I burst out laughing.

"You've got to be kidding me!" I blurted when I stopped laughing. "You want me to go all the way to Boston to a Chinese laundry? Is that the best you can come up with?"

He stared at me with a stern look, his deep brown eyes not blinking. He didn't say a word just stared at me.

"Okay, what's the catch? I mean this is some kind of joke, right? Is this one of those crazy prank shows or something?"

He reached into his pocket and pulled out an envelope. "I assure you, this is no joke. Look at these pictures closely before you say anything more."

I snatched the papers from his outstretched hand and glanced at them. They were photographs of my family, and more importantly, of me standing in front of a building that, as of that moment, was only a proposal to be built. Another one showed an obituary in the local newspaper with my picture and name and all the information to go with it.

The more I thought about the story being absolutely ridiculous, the more I thought of my grandmother and her stories and my fascination grew. Trying not to show my eagerness, I asked calmly, "So what's going on?"

He cleared his throat twice before speaking. "Two days ago, you brought a shirt to

Ideal Laundry for Mrs. Clark that was to be cleaned, pressed and starched."

"Yeah, so what?" I remarked.

He shot me a look like a father gives an errant child.

"Sorry," I apologized and motioned for him to continue.

His face softened a little but his tone was still serious. "Ideal sends their special laundry items to Ho Ling's in Chinatown which is why it takes them a couple days to get them finished. You will need the ticket for the shirt. Without it, you will only waste your time and come back empty-handed, like you did the first time."

"Whoa. Whoa. Like I did the first time? What the hell are you talking about?"

"This is the third time you have had to do this because you keep thinking it's an elaborate joke."

I started to protest, but he immediately flicked his hand to shut me up, and like an obedient child, I did.

Satisfied he had my attention again, he continued, "However, this is going to be your last chance. Should you ignore this warning or fail to do as you are instructed, you will die, make no mistake about it."

My head was spinning. I shook it to clear my thoughts. "Who are you?"

"I'm not at liberty to say, except to tell you what you need to know."

His eyes set, he motioned with his head. "Shall I continue?"

"Yeah, sure," I replied throwing my hands up.

He gave a satisfactory nod. "The shirt belongs to Mrs. Clark's son, Donald. Donald is…..well, to put it mildly, daffy. Ever since his father, who by the way, was an alcoholic, and had run off with some other woman, leaving Mrs. Clark and Donald to fend for themselves, Donald has never been right. He has been a misfit his whole life and is like a stick of dynamite ready to explode.

"The shirt happens to be his favorite and he is planning on wearing it to a concert in the park on Saturday night. Because his mother gave you the shirt and because you were the one to bring it to the laundry, Donald blamed you both and thus killed the two of you."

"He killed me?" I asked incredulously. "Well…I'll just call the police and tell them and there'll be nothing to worry about," I smirked.

"Wrong. What will you tell them? That this person is going to kill you because you brought his shirt to the laundry? Listen to how that sounds! Not only that, you tried doing that the first time and all it did was put Donald on alert. Don't be foolish, Carmen, this is your last chance or you will die once and for all."

With that, he looked down at his watch and stood up. "Pay attention to this warning if you truly want to continue living."

I walked him to the door not knowing what to think.

"Have a good day, Carmen, and should you heed my words, you will have a good life ahead of you. Goodbye."

"Goodbye," I said robotically and watched him until he disappeared around the corner.

I closed the door and headed for the small living room where I sat in the glider rocker. Whenever things get a little much for me, I sit in the rocker and let my mind and body relax. The gliding motion has a soothing effect on me. I pondered the man's words over again trying to make sense…future…shirt…laundry…Donald…I'm not sure how much time passed before the man's words finally began to unscramble themselves in my mind.

"Am I dreaming? Dead? A spirit with no body? If I died the first time, how did I come back to life again? Did I really die? And what happened the second time?" The whole thing was crazier than the tales my grandmother shared with me. I couldn't help but feel like I was waiting for the dream or nightmare to end so I could get back to my normal life. More questions inundated my mind. "Should I ignore the guy? What if he was telling the truth? Would I really die?"

At some point, I fell into a deep slumber in the rocker and woke up late the next morning. I went into the kitchen and made a cup of coffee. I sat down at the table and spotted the piece of paper with the poem on it. I picked it up and read it and realized I hadn't been a dreaming at all. The problem had worked itself out in my sleep and I knew what I had to do.

I got dressed and made the trek to China Town in Boston to get Donald's shirt from Ho Ling's. Then I dropped it off at his mother's house in time for him to wear it to the concert. As it turned out, the whole incident was neither a dream nor a nightmare, but, in fact, inexplicably real.

Apparently, Donald was deranged. He did go on a shooting spree at the concert. Fortunately, he was a lousy shot and no one was killed. But, a number of people were wounded, mostly with minor injuries. A few suffered serious injuries and were treated at the emergency room and released within a week.

My life was changed from that moment on. Not a day goes by that I don't think about what happened or about my grandmother.

Maybe she played some part in it. After all, she must have had an inkling that all the strange unexplainable things she had shared with me growing up would teach me to trust and follow my intuition.

Needless to say, whether that is an accurate case of reasoning or not, I am grateful for each and every day, and I am truly grateful that my grandmother loved and trusted me enough to share her life's experiences with me.

Changing Moments

Stepping from the Weller and Wheir office building, Paul Callan and Mark Jannitz turned to the right. Sitting on the ground was a young girl, a blanket wrapped snuggly around her. She wore a sign hanging from a string around her neck pleading for donations and held a small cup in her tiny hand.

Mark reached into his pocket, pulled out a bill and placed it in the cup.

"God bless you," the girl smiled and looked toward Paul who turned and quickly walked away.

"Why do you encourage her?" he asked when Mark caught up to him.

"I'm not encouraging her," Mark replied. "She's just a kid. Who knows what her situation is that's got her out here begging."

Paul looked at him. "Don't be so damn naïve all the time. She's probably out here because her mother's at home with a bunch of illegitimate kids and doesn't get enough from welfare. Trust me, you're not helping her. Whether you realize it or not, you're enabling her."

Mark shook his head. "Why are you so bitter and callous?"

Paul avoided answering. Inside the restaurant, he said, "We need to get moving on this project or we'll both be sucking our thumbs if the jungle drums are right."

"Have you heard any more about whether the company is going to close or just down-size?" Mark asked a tone of dread in his voice.

"Not a thing," Paul replied shaking his head. "I believe I have enough years to keep me locked in if they have cutbacks."

Mark cleared his throat. "I don't want to sound like I'm having second thoughts, but are you certain this concept of ours will hold water?"

Paul stared into Mark's eyes. "That's what I wanted to talk to you about. I've been testing the waters and I already have a few companies who are interested in marketing their services with us. They believe our marketing strategies are the best they've seen in years."

Mark took a deep breath and sighed. "It's going to take a lot of capital to get this off the ground. I mean, I'm risking everything."

Paul nodded. "I know that. Look, we've been friends for years. I'm not going to send you to the poor farm like that kid we just passed."

The men continued talking while eating their meal and then headed back to the office. Neither of them noticed the young girl was no longer sitting in front of the building.

After the two men had come out of the building and were out of sight, Sandy decided to leave. She struggled to her feet and winced. The pain in her leg was acting up more than usual. She had injured the leg falling off her bike months before and, because she didn't have insurance or money to cover medical costs, it didn't heal right. It made her leg look deformed.

She counted the money in the cup. She had $4.18. It was enough to get a burger and a drink and a little left over for breakfast the next morning. Talking to one of the cleaning ladies who worked in the office building, Sandy learned that the taller of the two men was named, Paul. Mark was the name of the shorter man. He was the one who was always nice to her.

When Sandy reached the house where she was living, she hesitated before entering. She looked around and, confidant no one was nearby, she crawled behind a forsythia bush to a small wooden door. She learned that at one time, the door had been used for coal deliveries. It was only by accident that she discovered the door when one day she kicked an empty can that was on the sidewalk and it ricocheted off the fence and rolled behind the bush. At first, she was going to leave the can and walk away, but guilt set in. She knew the right thing to do was go and get it. Down on hands and knees, she worked her way behind the bush and that's when she discovered the door.

Sandy remembered studying the door for a few moments before giving it a push with her hands. It didn't open. She tried again and again, but failed to get it open. Not one to give up easily, Sandy turned onto her side facing away from the door and, with a thrust of her butt, knocked the door open. Because the forsythia bush and her body were blocking any substantial light from shining into the dark interior, Sandy was unable to determine what lie beyond.

She eased out from behind the bush. Before standing up, she made sure no one was around and then headed down the street. The next day, Sandy waited until it was dark before she made her way back to the house with the small door. Once behind the forsythia bush, she eased the small door open, stretched her arm out and clicked on the flashlight she remembered to bring with her. She stuck her head inside to have a look around.

The room wasn't large, but offered enough space for her to live in. The back of the room was to her right and had a stone platform high enough off the ground and wide enough for her to make a bed. To the left was a door that looked to be secured. A recessed area in the far wall would serve as a good place to put up a clothesline. The rest she would work out once she moved her belongings in. She smiled knowing she would no longer have to deal with the other homeless kids who were always trying to steal her things or her money. She also relished the thought of not having to fight some of the older kids who always called her a freak and beat her up. They knew that underneath her clothes was really a boy's body. One of the boys had seen her washing up one day and told the others. After that, her daily life was a nightmare because she never knew when the next round of trouble would come.

Two months after moving into the basement, Sandy returned home to find a surprise waiting for her. In spite of her vigilance to make certain no one knew what she was doing, someone had discovered her secret. Climbing down the three-step ladder she had purchased at the second hand store, she turned on the small battery operated lantern she had bought. On the small table she had also purchased at the same second hand store, were a sandwich and a small bottle of milk.

She panicked and started gathering her clothes to leave. That is, until it dawned on her that whoever it was who knew she was there and left her the food, had to be okay with her living there. Sandy put the clothes she had snatched up onto her bed and sat down. It had to be someone who lived in the house above. She had no idea who it could be, but she was determined to find out.

One night, Sandy left the house as usual, but instead of going anywhere, she doubled back just out of sight. Positive no one was looking, she scurried back to the forsythia bush. Sandy crawled behind it and carefully eased the door open just far enough to peek in. Not long after, she watched as the secured cellar door to the room opened and the elderly lady who lived on the first floor entered. The lady placed the wrapped sandwich and drink on the table and left, locking the door behind her.

The following morning, Sandy checked the mailboxes and learned the lady's name was Mrs. Birges. A week later, with flowers in hand, Sandy knocked on Mrs. Birges' door. When Mrs. Birges opened the door, Sandy handed her the flowers and said, "Thank you for the food and drinks."

Sandy recalled the warm, gentle smile on Mrs. Birges' face when she had handed the flowers to her. The memories flooded her head. That was the moment when Mrs. Birges invited her in and they became friends. Mrs. Birges was actually more than just a friend, she was the closest thing to the grandmother Sandy always dreamed of having.

Four months after Paul and Mark first spoke about the company downsizing, Mark got his notice that he was being let go. He walked into Paul's office holding the slip up for Paul to see.

Paul stood up and walked around to the front of the desk. "I'm sorry. I heard the news about three minutes before you got called into the conference room." Seeing the worried looked on Mark's face, he added, "We'll be okay. I'll make some phone calls this afternoon to see if I can get some appointments set up."

At the end of the day, upset that he failed to get any definite appointments, Paul left the office in a bad mood. Outside, he spotted the little girl sitting where she had been many days before. When she looked up at him, he said, "Why don't you go home and tell your mother to get a job."

In spite of the hurt reflecting in her eyes, she still managed to smile at him and say, "Have a nice day."

For the next few weeks, regardless of what time he entered or left the Weller & Wheir office building, Paul was confronted by the girl collecting donations. Each day she would wish him a good day and, each time, he would grunt and walk past her. Sometimes he said cruel things to her.

A month after Mark's dismissal, Paul was given his termination papers and packed up his personal belongings and carried them out of the building.

The girl was sitting in her usual spot, but instead of wishing him a good day, she simply said, "You know you shouldn't be so angry all the time."

That got his attention and he stopped and looked down at her with a scowl. "How old are you?"

"I'm 12," she answered, staring him straight in the eyes.

"You're 12, huh? Let me tell you something. You're not old enough to be giving me advice. When you get old enough and have to work for a living instead of panhandling, then you'll know what the hardships in life are all about. Let's see if you're so happy then."

At that, she smiled her usual smile and said, "Have a nice day."

He shrugged his shoulders and stormed away. "Stupid kid," he mumbled under his breath.

The very next morning, Paul and Mark got their first big break and landed an account. From that moment on they seemed to be in a whirlwind of events. Ironically, they were able to get a large office in the Weller & Wheir office building just four floors down from their former employer. They were on their way.

Each day, they encountered the girl and each day, Mark gave her money. Of course, Paul voiced his opinions and objections and ignored the young girl's wishes to have a good day.

As the days passed, Paul realized he hadn't seen the girl sitting outside the office building collecting money. Finally, he made mention to Mark as they were going to lunch. "I see your friend hasn't been coming around."

Mark looked at him questioningly.

"The beggar," Paul supplied.

Mark glanced down and then looked around. "You're right," he said. "I wonder what happened to her."

"The cops probably nabbed her for vagrancy."

Mark just shook his head and continued walking toward the restaurant.

At lunch the next day, Mark stated, "I found out the kid's in the hospital."

"How'd you find that out?"

"I asked one of the cleaning girls if she knew anything about her."

"She's probably got pneumonia from sitting out here on the ground," Paul added with not an ounce of compassion in his voice.

Once again, Mark stared at his friend, trying to fathom why Paul was so cold and uncaring. But not being one to pry, he let the moment pass and they continued to the restaurant.

At the end of the day, Paul told Mark he was going to stay a little later to work on a layout for a new account they had acquired. Before long, the cleaning ladies came in and Paul asked one of them if she knew the hospital to which the girl had been taken. She didn't know, but returned a few minutes later with the information she had gotten from one of the other ladies.

Without knowing the girl's last name, and not being a relative, it took a bit of doing before he was able to find out what room she was in. She was in the Intensive Care Unit. It took even more convincing and pleading with the nurse in charge of the ICU to give him any information or allow him to visit.

"She's a homeless kid," the nurse supplied.

"Thank you," Paul nodded and started to walk away. He stopped and turned. "Can you tell me just how bad she is?"

The nurse shook her head, "It's hard to say other than she's in critical condition."

When the nurse brought Paul into the room, he asked, "Do you know if her mother has been informed?"

The nurse looked at him sadly, "The police told us she has no family. Her father left her and her mother when she was a baby, and was killed in a car accident sometime later. Her mother passed away when Sandra was 10 years old."

As happy as Sandy was with having Mrs. Birges as a friend, she was never able to tell Mrs. Birges who she really was or how sad she really felt inside. She was deeply depressed because in her heart, she believed she would never be able to become the real girl she knew she was meant to be. It was on such a morning of feeling deep sadness that Sandy attempted to make things physically right.

It was only by chance that Mrs. Birges had finished washing and drying Sandy's clothes that morning. When she entered the room where Sandy stayed, she noticed her on the bed. When she went to see if she was okay, Mrs. Birges sucked in her breath and said, "Oh my God. No, this can't be happening." She hurried up stairs and called the fire department emergency number.

The paramedics and the police showed up within minutes and took Sandy to the hospital. The police remained behind gathering as much information as they could from Mrs. Birges. She told them everything Sandy had shared with her.

Paul lowered his head then tilted it to look at the nurse. "So what actually happened to bring her here? Is it pneumonia?"

Clearing her throat, the nurse whispered, "She mutilated herself."

Paul was confused. "What do you mean….she cut her wrists?" He glanced at Sandra's arms. There were no bandages on her wrists.

As she moved to the opposite side of the bed to adjust the covers, the nurse said, "She tried to make herself into a girl."

Horrified by the news, Paul clamped his hand over his mouth and closed his eyes. He couldn't believe it. He didn't want to believe it. It couldn't be happening a second time to him.

"Are you okay?" the nurse asked when she came to the side of the bed where Paul was seated.

He didn't answer or look at her, just nodded.

As the nurse was checking the tubes connected to Sandra's arms, Paul noticed that one of Sandra's legs was misshapen.

When the nurse left the room, Paul buried his face in his hands. His words about knowing life's hardships returned to haunt him. Having lost his own daughter, Tina, who committed suicide when she was just 14 years old, he had turned bitter and resentful. When Tina told him she was really a boy and wanted to have the surgeries, he screamed and yelled at her. He called her a freak and an abomination. He said he wished she had never been born. He berated his wife until she couldn't take it anymore and his marriage broke up. After that, he never allowed himself to get involved with anyone on an intimate basis. Instead, he suffered in his loneliness in spite of having had the means to overcome it.

Now, as he sat in the hospital room, with the monitors beeping, he realized that he knew absolutely nothing about real loneliness. Sandra, on the other hand, did. Yet, in spite of all she had lost and been through, she still smiled and offered a blessing.

He now understood that her panhandling was a way to stay alive. The cruel words he had spat at her on so many days invaded his mind and tore at his heart. What kind of a monster had he become?

"I'm sorry," the nurse's voice interrupted his thoughts. "Your 15 minutes are over."

Paul glanced at Sandra and then at the nurse and nodded. He stood up feeling like all the energy in his body had completely drained out of him. He was a shell moving robotically toward the door. In the elevator, he vowed to return and to speak to the doctors to find out what could be done to help Sandra.

That night, Paul had difficulty falling asleep. Tortured by the memories of Tina and the visions of Sandra lying in the bed hooked up to machines, he tossed and turned until he passed out from emotional exhaustion.

His concentration in the office the next morning was anything but focused. At lunch, he explained to Mark about Tina and his visit to see Sandra the night before. Mark sat quietly while Paul informed him of Tina's death and Sandra's deformed leg and being hooked up to the monitors.

Mark was then able to understand why Paul had a cold attitude. He sympathized with all that his friend had gone through. Having children of his own, Mark also shivered at the thought of losing one of them. Such pain was beyond his comprehension. He wondered if he could have endured for so long without having to shut his emotions off.

After lunch, Mark headed back to the office while Paul hailed a taxi to go to the

hospital. He was determined to find a way to help Sandra. In an effort to overcome the mounting fear of witnessing another child's death by her own hand, Paul considered a number of scenarios that would make things right. Most of the ideas he dismissed almost as quickly as he thought of them. One thought, however, weaved in and out of his mind until it finally stood out above the others. He strongly believed that adopting Sandra was the right decision to make. He kept thinking that their meeting was more by design than happenstance.

At the hospital, Paul forced himself to remain patient and calm as the elevator seemed to take forever to open. He made his way to the nurse's station. He asked if the doctor had been in and how Sandra was doing. The nurse informed him the doctor would be with him shortly and told Paul he could go in to see Sandra.

Paul reached out and took Sandra's hand in his own and was shocked at how cold it felt. He put his other hand over hers and whispered, "It's going to be okay. I'll keep you warm. I'm so sorry for all the things I said to you and one day I'll explain why I was so cold and nasty toward you."

One of the monitors in the room started beeping loudly and two nurses came running into the room. One of the nurses came to the side of the bed where Paul was standing. "There's a small room down the corridor. Once we see what's going on, we'll let you come back in."

Paul reluctantly walked to the small family waiting room. He sat down and closed his eyes.

A short time later, the door opened and a man came in. "Hello, I'm Dr. Sinchow," he introduced himself.

Paul stood up. "Can you tell me what's wrong with Sandra and what can be done to get her back to good health?"

Dr. Sinchow cleared his throat. "I'm afraid that it's going to be touch and go for Sandra for the next several hours," he offered somberly.

The words startled Paul. "Her condition's that bad?"

Dr. Sinchow lowered his eyes then looked at Paul. "She tried to cut her penis off and nearly succeeded. She's lost a lot of blood. We're doing everything we can, but a lot is going to depend on whether Sandra fights to stay alive or not."

Paul felt his knees weaken and sat down. Pent up tears flowed down his cheeks. A number of things raced into his mind, but none of them coalesced into a coherent thought.

Just then, Dr. Sinchow's pager beeped. He glanced down at Paul and said, "You can go in to see her if you're up to it. I'll tell the nurses." He then left the room. Moments later, a nurse appeared and asked Paul if he was okay and whether he wanted some water. He shook his head and whispered, "No. Thank you. Can I go in now?"

The nurse nodded. "Yes, come with me."

Paul stood by the bed hating the fact that once again there was nothing he could do. His heart was breaking. He reached down and held Sandra's hand. "I don't know if you can hear me, Sandra, but I'm the man who treated you badly when I would come out of the office at Weller & Wheir every day. Please forgive me for my stupidity."

He stretched a leg out and hooked his foot behind the rung of the chair, pulled it closer and sat down. He bowed his head and closed his eyes, wishing with all his heart that she would be all right, yet knowing that his wishes might not come true.

Paul wasn't sure how long he had been there but he heard Sandra give a deep sigh and the monitor flat lined. He knew she had died. When the nurses came running in, he was still holding Sandra's hand. His cheeks were stained with tears.

"You have to leave," the nurse commanded.

As Paul exited the room, Dr. Sinchow and other medical personnel rushed into the room. He wasn't sure what to do. Part of him wanted to stay in hopes Sandra would pull through, while the other part of him didn't want to face watching another child die. He made it to the elevator, but before the doors opened, he turned and went into the small waiting room where he paced back and forth for what seemed an eternity. He closed his left hand and wrapped his right hand around it and held them up to his chest. "Please don't let her die," he whispered over and over again.

Paul heard movement behind him and turned to see Dr. Sinchow standing near the door. At first, Paul couldn't tell by Dr. Sinchow's face if the news was good or bad. He took a deep breath and waited.

Dr. Sinchow stepped into the room and smiled, "It was touch and go there for a while but we saved her. She's resting now. Paul breathed a sigh of relief upon hearing the good news.

"The nurse told me that you are thinking about adopting Sandra?" Dr. Sinchow said.

"Yes, I am considering that."

"May I ask why?" Dr. Sinchow asked.

Paul explained what had happened to his daughter.

Dr. Sinchow pointed to the chairs and both men sat down. "Adopting someone to ease your guilt is not the best reason to go through with such a thing. You do realize that Sandra is going to need a lot of medical care, as well as counseling to deal with her gender issues? Aside from the expenses she'll accrue, she's also going to need lots of support and, more importantly, a good home and lots of love. Have you thought about all that, Mr. Callan?"

Paul ran his fingers through his hair and glanced out the window.

Dr. Sinchow stood up. "You don't have to make that decision right now, but I strongly suggest you consider all of that before you make a choice that might destroy that young girl's life more than what it has been destroyed already." Before stepping out of the room, he added, "You can go in to see her, but only for five minutes."

Paul nodded. "Thank you." He stood up and walked slowly toward Sandra's room. Before entering, he paused in the doorway and breathed deeply to brace himself. Sandra looked so fragile in the bed and Paul had all he could do to keep the tears from flowing again. He pulled the chair closer to the bed and took Sandra's hand in his.

"I'm not sure you can hear me," he started, "but I swear to you that I'm going to give you a beautiful home. I'm also going to make it possible for you to get all the surgeries you need to be the beautiful girl you are."

At that moment, the nurse appeared at the door. "I'm sorry but you'll have to leave."

Paul got up and placed Sandra's hand by her side. "I'll be back tomorrow."

Paul left the hospital. Instead of hailing a taxi, he decided to walk back to the office. As he walked, Sandra's words burned in his mind, "You shouldn't be so angry all the time." He took a deep breath and knew in his heart that his life would be changed forever. It would be a change for the better because that's how Tina and Sandra would want it to be.

Exactly one year to the day from when Paul made the promise to give Sandra a new home, the adoption papers were signed. During that year, Sandra was enrolled in school and had the necessary surgery to correct her deformed leg. Every week she met with a gender therapist to prepare her for gender affirmation surgery.

The day of the adoption, Paul held a party for Sandra. Mark came with his wife and children. Paul also invited some of his other close friends and their children as well as the cleaning ladies from the office building who had befriended Sandra. As a very special surprise, Paul invited Mrs. Birges to join them.

At the end of the day, when Sandra was ready for bed, Paul said, "I'm not angry anymore. I have a special daughter now who I love very much."

Sandra kissed him on the cheek and smiled. She climbed into bed and replied, "I'm not sad anymore. I love you. Good night, Dad."

Paul was so moved at the sound of those words, tears streamed down his cheeks. Before Sandra could see them, he turned off the light and said, "Goodnight Sandy."

BOOKS PUBLISHED BY TRANSGRESS PRESS

Vicissitudes
Kim Green

Tomorrow, or Forever
And Other Stories
Jack Kaulfus

Swimming Upstream: A Novel
Jacob Anderson-Minshall

Lou Sullivan
Daring To Be A Man Among Men
Brice D. Smith

American Fascism: How the GOP is Subverting Deomcracy
Brynn Tannehill

Giving It Raw: Nearly 30 Years with AIDS
Francisco Ibañez-Carrasco

Life Beyond My Body
Transgender Journey to Manhood in China
Lei Ming

Below the Belt: Genital Talk by Men of Trans Experience
Edited by Trystan Theosophus cotton

Trunky (Transgender Junky)
A Memoir of Institutionalization and Southern Hospitality
Sam Peterson

Queer Rock Love: A Family Memoir
Paige Schilt

Love Always
Partners of Trans People on Intimacy, Challenge, and Resilience
Edited by Jordon Johnson and Becky Garrison

Now What?
A Handbook for Families with Transgender Children
Rex Butt

Trans Homo...Gasp! Gay FTM and Cis Men on Sex and Love
Edited by Avi Ben-Zeev and Pete Bailey

New Girl Blues...or Pinks
Mary Degroat Ross

Letters for My Sisters: Transitional Wisdom in Retrospect
Edited by Andrea James and Deanne Thornton

Manning Up: Transsexual Men on
Finding Brotherhood, Family and Themselves
Edited by Zander Keig and Mitch Kellaway

Hung Jury: Testimonies of Genital Surgery by Transsexual Men
Edited by Trystan Theosophus Cotten

Words of Fire!
Women Loving Women in Latin America
Antonia Amprino

The Wanderings of Chela Coatlicue
On Tour with Los Huerfanos
Ananda Esteva

Made in the USA
Middletown, DE
20 July 2021

44430760R00057